The Cherokee Promise

Rebuilding Humanity after the Fall

A. O. Huddleston

Table of Contents

Copyright

Published by Defiance Press & Publishing, LLC
Bulk orders of this book may be obtained by contacting Defiance Press & Publishing, LLC. www.defiancepress.com.
Defiance Press & Publishing, LLC
281-581-9300
info@defiancepress.com

Like now a filthy bird descends on any,
Rotting carcass, the dead, the many,
Who lived once, caused a freedom stir,
Now her blood clots, settles inside her.

Chapter 1

His parents named him Jeremiah, and it has been thirty years since his birth.

"Oh, no," the two words came out of the son as a reflex, much like the opening notes of a slow blues song. The night's sleep had been short again. He was alone with his dog, and another day of survival lay ahead for both of them in search of food and water. It had been the same routine for them since that long day of harsh light—the day the world became foreign to those still alive. The hours when last names became far less important.

Water quickly became a precious resource. Food was difficult to come by and hard to find. Without water, it mattered less. Whatever water Jeremiah found could be made safe by boiling and stored in various clean bottles that served as canteens. One of these was an old plastic canteen, military issue, with a stainless steel cup. The canteen could still nestle snugly in a threadbare nylon pouch. These canteens were very important to Jeremiah and were protected as much as one protects money or jewelry.

Part of his daily job was to protect his dog, a companion he had treasured for nine years. He sometimes wondered aloud to the dog if it was returning his loyalty by protecting him. The dog was a mixed breed, about seventy pounds, with longer white fur that had patches and specks of black and brown. He had one blue eye and one brown eye. He was a lucky one because Jeremiah had saved him from the cooking fires of other survivors when he was a pup. He named the spirited dog Jack.

Jeremiah had to wake up and be on guard. He sat up with a groan, reached for a water bottle, took a long drink, and thought about how great a cup of coffee would taste if he had it. After packing up the gear and supplies, he would set about finding their daily provisions. Some days there was nothing; other days they were fortunate. A squirrel here, a rabbit there, and maybe some indistinguishable berries—most of which didn't cause a violent reaction in his stomach—and could still be found from the new shoots beginning to grow on nearby mountain slopes rising up from the road since that day. Some berries did cause him to retch, though. He learned that it was easier to eat his vomit off the ground than to smooth the swallow.

He came to know that most humans who survived the nuclear blasts had devolved into stalking and killing any living creature they could use as food. Jeremiah knew that Jack was food to them. He had an old .44 Magnum pistol and a few boxes of ammunition for Jack's and his own protection. Most of the time, merely showing the piece was enough to dissuade those with bad intentions from moving on—somewhere else, likely to steal from others one way or another, but away from him and Jack. The dog was born in the early days when the earth was beginning to rebirth.

The stench of death still came with the winds across the countryside in waves. Stronger from the north as the winds blew southerly, but it always came regardless of where the wind carried itself. It blew in from every direction; at times, there were different levels of odor riding the winds, much like a hijacker that came almost constantly. The smell was an unwanted, filthy, and constant reminder of the state life had become. Life was no more than survival. Much of the earth remained charred remnants of great fires. It was as if the fire consumed its surface and boiled waters near the centers of those lights. There was little left that resembled the country of the past. Jeremiah remembered little of that life.

He shook his head, rubbed his eyes, and called out, "Jack!" The dog always came to him, his mouth open and tail wagging quickly back and forth. The dog knew nothing else. Finding Jack enough food was as difficult as finding himself enough to have the strength to stand. He knew he had to move into another area but had no idea where to go. At a distance, he visited the new growth in the mountains, but it was still only small shoots. It was in the forest on the hills that made up the mountains where he found most of the berries and occasional meat.

The shack he found a few years ago had been good enough to keep them warm in the winter and hidden from the sun in the summers, but the food and water sources had been used up. There had been less and less, and this morning he woke up not knowing where to begin his search. It seemed the food was all gone.

Others who passed close by had simply used most of it up. The shack was a mile from the main road, which, although old, buckled, and cracked, had served as one of the thoroughfares people in search of food, water, and shelter used. This one was east of old Chattanooga and well north of burned-out Atlanta—at the furthest point of Georgia on the border of what was once known as North Carolina. These places were known by Jeremiah's parents, though he barely related to the names of places or that much about them. He knew what a pistol was—one of his father's legacies left for him after teaching him how to use it, maintain it, and repair it if he had to. He taught Jeremiah to shoot, too, and explained the importance of being ready and able to use it on anything or anyone threatening him.

The road that crossed the countryside in front of his shack was used by people going south or north in their own search for life. Along the way, they all used whatever they could find. Jeremiah understood that and didn't blame them unless they attacked him or Jack.

Suddenly, he thought he heard quiet movement. It could be food. Alone with Jack, he concentrated on following the sound and carefully moved toward it by sliding closer to the source. He couldn't make it out exactly, and it came scattered, without a constant rhythm—as if something was trying to be stealthy but not quite pulling it off just outside his home. He quietly reached for his .44 and held it against his chest, a small, almost concave part of him these days. He eyed Jack as if to tell the dog to be still and quiet while he determined what the sound was outside stalking them. Jack had no fear of other men, and he heard the sound a second time, standing alert. The dog was ready for food or other men and began to run.

Jeremiah quickly jumped to his feet and followed Jack as he barked at a visitor. He felt his eyes furrow with determination. It may be an animal or the most dangerous creature, a human, and he had to be ready. The last time he confronted one of these killers was over a year ago, and he had to shoot him square in the chest to stop him. He buried the man in the back field, far enough away from the shack where weeds had finally begun to grow tall enough to hide the result that still haunted him.

A stranger suddenly appeared out of the shadows and came at him with a machete. The man wore shredded clothing, the appearance of evil in his red eyes, his mouth open slightly and stretched toward the back of his thin neck, showing hatred and hunger. He was going to kill Jeremiah to get the dog or both of them.

Jeremiah knew it was time for him and Jack to move on and find another home. This was one too many unwanted visitors, he thought. As he ran outside, he saw the figure strike Jack with something before he could stop him, causing the dog to yelp in pain. Without thinking, he leveled the pistol toward the darkly covered, bearded, filthy man.

"Stop right there!" Jeremiah found a heavy voice pushing the words up from his diaphragm. "I'll shoot you dead where you stand. Back off! Drop that machete you're holding!"

"Please, mister, I mean no harm," a gravelly voice came out from beneath the hair and crust.

"Jack! Come to me!" Jeremiah called out to his dog. "You're a liar. You're a damned liar!" he said as he fixed his aim on the center of the man's chest.

"Just let me go, mister. I won't bother you and the dog."

"Leave now and I won't shoot you."

After watching the figure disappear into the horizon, he knelt by Jack to assess the damage. At least the dog wasn't bleeding, so he thought Jack had a good chance of coming out of this encounter well. If Jack hadn't feared others because of his protection before today, he would now. Maybe something good has come out of this, he thought as he sucked back sinus and tears when he saw that Jack's front left leg might be broken because he yelped in pain at his touch. The son of a son is lucky. If I had known this, I would have shot him in his left leg, he thought at first and then corrected himself, no, that would have been a death sentence.

He slowly and carefully manipulated the dog's leg to reset the bone but could not do so without hurting him a little more than he already was. He set the leg with a splint and some duct tape he had. He finished the wrap by using an old shirt he tore into strips for ties. There was nothing he could do to ease the dog's pain. Jack was going through something akin to what he remembered experiencing when he injured himself a couple of times. Natural healing was all there was to rely on.

Jeremiah knew he had to leave his shack sooner than he had planned. The number of people passing on the road had increased, and he was certain it would become worse. The man he let go knew there was food in his place, and to protect Jack, he needed to put distance between the shack and any strangers. His first idea was to walk further up the base slope of the mountains, where he and Jack had foraged for berries and small animals many times. There was some cover there, and it would serve them well for the first couple of miles. The stranger may have friends, and at night, they could visit the shack and take their chances to get a meal of dog.

We can stay the night that far away and then try to make it over the mountain in the morning and on toward the larger slopes, he thought as he began to rig up a litter for Jack to lie on while he pulled him and the few supplies he quickly gathered. He took a last look at the shack and felt he was leaving something of value. He and Jack had to move on and find a different place. He remembered the words seared into his memory, Whatever is ahead of you, son, go into it with the faith that you can handle anything that comes your way. Be determined, strong, and take up the challenge. You do that, and you will make it through the hell we see before us in this terrible time. If anything should happen to us, remember your mom and me. We'll be with you every step. You won't see us, but you'll feel us. You will know we are that part of you that makes you take the next step. The last few words he heard his father say before he heard his parents' workplace was destroyed. They knew the times were dangerous back then and still worked to provide for a young boy. They succeeded in protecting their son but were taken by the blast nearby. Their memory returned to him each time he needed them.

Only later did he understand the reason they both stepped out that day, the day filled with distant lights and wind. That day of explosive noise was unlike anything heard by most people on Earth before or since. They had to work to provide for their son and themselves. It was as simple as that. He cared for and watched his parents in his early years and knew they were forever gone.

He knew the face of the mountain nearest his shack very well—from about two miles to the north and from the mile to the south that ended within five hundred yards of his road as it wound its way up from Atlanta. He thought about going down there on occasion to see if there was anything left and if maybe there were people who did not want to eat his dog. It had been too great a chance to take. He put those thoughts aside when he looked at Jack.

He remembered his father working in construction but didn't know everything he was capable of. He recalled going to school and making it to the tenth grade before that day. That day everything changed. There were no answers as to why the powers unleashed upon each other the deadliest force—they killed millions. He remembered there were no smiles and no laughter any longer with so many taken so quickly. Jeremiah lost all his friends and then saw a town and countryside littered with bodies. Before that day, there had been smiles and laughter and a generally good living for everyone he knew. Now there were none of those things.

Dragging the litter with Jack resting behind him, he began the walk at dusk while keeping a keen eye on his surroundings to ensure no one saw him. At first, Jack didn't want to ride, and Jeremiah had to tie him down. He strapped the dog's stomach and rear legs so he couldn't try to jump off and injure his leg worse. Jack looked confused and then settled into a stare as just ahead of him, Jeremiah took determined quick steps, one after another. The mountain was one of Jack's favorite places after all, and he knew the direction. He thought that after Jack recovered in the mountains, he could run and hunt, jump onto Jeremiah in sheer joy, and enjoy himself. Jeremiah hoped for darkness soon, where he could walk another few miles to ensure no one could find them.

He had heard rumors from a few passersby about people who lived beyond the mountain range he was familiar with over the years. An occasional friendly passerby would take a rest with him in his shack. He kept count on only two hands how many of these there were over twenty years. The idea that there could be a germ of civilization did his mind and heart good amid the constant fear of most of the survivors he encountered. He didn't know whether it was true or not, and if it was, he couldn't be sure they were friendly. He did not know the distance or the best direction to take.

Dusk was soon overcome by night, and he could move well away from the road and the shack he left behind. He had enough of the place. He had enough of the risk; the desperation of the survivors had become more acute than even it was immediately after those days of heat and light. That was when most death revealed itself. Afterward, there was a steady loss of human beings for years by nature through murder or simple starvation. The odor that rode in the winds would be part of his experience for a while yet, he figured.

He knew he'd been fortunate. Just when he began to feel too weak to carry on, he'd found something for him and Jack to eat—he knew it was the divine that saw them through those days. Having been taught about God by his parents and instructed how to pray, he knew what they taught him was truer than anything others had told him. He saw the tail end of a snake moving away from him. It was easy to catch and kill for food. Jeremiah always remembered to be thankful, though his prayers were most often silent, as they were for finding this snake. Still, he knew each prayer was heard. He cooked the snake over a fire for himself and Jack.

He listened for others as he walked up the slope, taking one step after another and not yielding to breath or exhaustion. It didn't matter how bad he felt or whether he was certain he could take another step without collapsing. He had to take the steps and keep taking them.

The red and orange glow of a full moon appeared in a full circle at midnight. He felt a measure of sweet freedom and took comfort in that knowledge. Freedom still had to be protected by the barrel of a gun. He remembered his mom and dad teaching him that people throughout history failed to realize over generations that their liberty was being taken away from them, ever so surely, ever so precisely. The erosion had emptied and destroyed the dream through his parents' time; the nation was very different and full of quarreling and greed. Little remained that resembled freedom as it was known in the United States for sporadic parts of her existence.

His parents stopped talking about what was happening because it hurt both of them so much to even think about it. Once other nations perceived weakness in the relatively new country of the United States, they must have strategized that the time was right to strike against her and take her down.

Chapter 2

He felt a gentle touch of moisture on his skin when he woke up in daylight. He wasn't sure where he was, but he had put enough distance between himself and the shack to keep Jack safe. He found a tangle of downed trees, long stripped bare of any leaves or new growth, but the rods of wood still provided him and Jack some shelter. He was somewhere near the top of the second mountain he had ventured onto the night before, on its opposite downslope, hidden away from any strange eyes. He could see the last mile ahead of him toward its crest. He could see green, and that meant many things were growing.

He tasted his own sweat and blood and spat it out quickly as he shook his head to wake up alert. Jack was lying beside him and not moving yet, but he could see that the dog was breathing.

Jeremiah poured a cup of water into Jack's bowl and took a couple of swallows himself. He then reached into the pack he carried on the litter and brought out a piece of the snake he had saved for both the dog and himself. Finding food along their path was a priority, and he didn't know what was available this far away.

Food was used up quickly in those days of great light; it was as if a plague of eaters shadowed the land, devouring everything possible. It didn't take long before the land seemed barren of virtually all food. He thought he was watching from inside a mirror, unable to scramble the same way, unable to step out and join the frenzy. He just watched as others consumed the land and took their portion of what was left, leaving nothing for anyone else, offering nothing to others. Some he saw. Most he never saw. They must have passed through the area, and now most of them contributed to the odor. The same thing must be happening across the entire world.

After checking the splint on Jack, he strapped everything down again on the litter and set out on his trek toward a new home. He stepped and climbed down to the second valley and saw there was more green than before, feeling the hope of his father fill him. *More distance and I'll find food,* he thought. Several hours passed when he faintly heard the unmistakable sound of flowing water.

"We're going toward it, Jack. Hang on," he said to the dog. "It sounds like there's plenty to drink down there."

He knew to be careful with any body of water. The sound he heard was a flow and might be safe. In most cases where there was water, there were rotting corpses and a putrid stench. One couldn't take it without dying a slow, painful death, suffering from an incurable sickness that turned one's stomach into knots, making the skin crawl with nerves on fire before death overtook the victim. Death was the only thing that brought relief. He then became another decaying addition to the water pool—a mixture of blood, pus, feces, and solid matter—or another skeleton piled on skeletons nearby. Jeremiah had seen so many that the sight of any kind of human remains no longer shocked him. He passed them as easily as he passed stones, burnt tree trunks, or hard-packed dirt on the trails.

In the mountains, it was better—cleaner. The blessing of new growth was quickly overtaking the former landscape of hopelessness and destruction. In so many years, nature would reclaim much of what she lost, at least in the areas where few men tread. The destroyed cities would become greener through vines and growth—those that could thrive through cracks in concrete, asphalt, and steel. The appearance of the cities remained desolate and mostly vacant.

He walked toward the sounds. There was a distinct rhythm of slightly higher pitches mixed with a constant wet flow. Along the way, the breeze moved through new growth with a diminutive hum. He was getting closer and began sweating around his wide-open eyes, nerves dancing. He could taste sweet relief. Where there was water, there was hope.

He stumbled down a furrow cut into the side of the second mountain and saw the stream. It was coming from a third mountain and running into the valley that separated the rises. His pace quickened, and Jack the dog held his head up high, turning his ear to align with the same sound. Jack began licking his mouth and barking.

The stream looked clean. He cupped his hands, smelled it, and tasted the water. Satisfied it wasn't contaminated, he let Jack off the leash so he could wade into the shallow, cool water on three legs and drink to his heart's content. Jeremiah filled every container he brought that would hold water for both of them and rested for an hour by the shallow bank.

He saw life in the water. *Unbelievable... there are minnows living!* He studied the lively scene. "It's a great sign the earth's returning," he said to Jack as if he could understand human words. Jack often surprised him, so he couldn't be sure the dog didn't know.

A pair of eyes were watching Jeremiah and Jack from a distance above them. Sitting as still as a tree on the third mountain, halfway up its northerly slope, a watcher kept them under surveillance. The tone of his skin and clothing blended with the colors of the land. His long black hair was tied back to keep his eyes clear. He had a rifle at his feet, loaded and ready.

The watcher was one of many people who had migrated to live in this mountain range from a place once known as North Carolina. Those who could left the area before the day of heat and light when the inevitable rolled over the country, as foretold by tribal elders. Although the citizens lost most of their number that day because they had come to doubt the elders, seventy-seven survived by staying in the mountains. They kept their home in these mountains where no one else ventured. In the nearly two decades since that day, their numbers had grown to ninety because each child born was considered blessed. Each birth was a human renewal with a future, along with the few travelers of good intentions who found safety with these spiritual people.

Jeremiah raised his head and took in more of the aroma this cleaner area offered freely. It was close to what he remembered from long ago. He closed his eyes and savored it for all it was worth, and it was worth everything to him. Jack and he had a good chance here, he figured. It was now a matter of how best to set up and build a shelter—and where. Finding food would require a daily journey, but he and Jack would have a place to return to and rest.

The watchful eyes belonged to a modern-day warrior of the Cherokee-Creek nation named Victor. Victor was ten years old on the day of light when they had to leave and bore the scars of burns across his back and arms. He and thirty-two other men and women formed the front line defense of the tribe and were willing to die to keep the nation safe.

It is for their children they watch. The world is different, smaller.

It is for their people they stand as vanguards against the dangers of the new world.

It is for God's will, as He would have it for them to live right.

Jeremiah looked at the taller trees across the valley. He thought that they must be higher than the ten feet he was accustomed to seeing where there were live trees. With his mouth open in wonderment, he planned to take Jack to the third mountain. He thought there was a good chance that where such growth existed, other life existed. *Jack and I will surely thrive over there!*

He watched as Jack placed all four legs in the water. It was as if Jack knew there were some healing properties in its clean presentation and that it might help him. He smiled at Jack and let him stay in it as long as he desired. Desire was an emotion he had given up, for the elements of most desires were no longer possible, and so it lay dormant, much like all those former people who were nothing anymore.

The village elders were waiting for more information on the stranger who had shown up closer than most outsiders had in the ten years since the people moved into the mountains, cut the fields, built their homes, and stored food for winter. The elders remembered what had transpired in those days when the world changed and foresaw it coming before their people could be trapped in its fire and death.

Jeremiah watched Jack and joined him in the rush of water and its pools formed wherever there were depressions. He smiled as he saw Jack having a great time dipping his head and shaking water off after each time. The dog was in a new place. He was able to move along on three legs, gently putting his fourth down to the earth every few steps, which was plenty to aid his spirit in this new recreation. It seemed that Jack was on the mend.

The warrior watched them with a steady brow and unmoving body. Nothing—not animal, bird, or man—could know he was there. It was part of his heritage and training as a young boy. He signaled to the watch nearest him with his hands, and the second watcher acted as a courier back to the village, where more of the people prepared themselves to deal with a possible threat.

The elders sent the patrol out to surround Jeremiah, with some walking east and others west, until there were twelve within one hundred yards of him. The signal came to close in on him.

Jeremiah had gotten out of the water and was lying nearby to dry before continuing the journey with Jack. He was opening one of his last cans of peaches when he sensed that he had company. He dropped the can opener and looked up to suddenly see the hardened, chiseled face of a muscled man holding a rifle on him. Jeremiah froze for a few seconds and didn't move any part of his body. Then another man appeared from somewhere, and before he could take more than three breaths, there were over a dozen armed men and women staring at him and Jack. He felt sick. Jack was surely going to die, and it was his fault for lingering too long in one place. He began to weep at the hopelessness of losing his only and best friend. Jack was an innocent creature whose only desire had been to always be a faithful companion, to fetch for him, to offer him plenty of licks on his long face when he felt down—and to take as long as it took to make Jeremiah speak and smile. He couldn't accept the thought of Jack being a meal and losing him that way.

Jeremiah's first impulse was to fight if necessary and die in his best effort to save Jack and himself. As he took a stance, ready to do what he could, one of the warriors stepped forward, closer. *It's my move. I'll grab his weapon and go for mine off the litter,* he thought.

"I am John. What brings you to this place?" the warrior said in a voice that Jeremiah could remember—a clear, distinct, strong voice—not the higher-pitched, broken kind of language that seemed to prevail in what was left of the world he knew. Jeremiah quickly decided to wait before he tried to lash out.

"I had to leave my home because Jack here would be eaten."

"He is safe here. What do you call yourself?"

"I am Jeremiah, named by my parents," he answered, feeling his eyes fill. "How do I know you speak the truth… that my partner here is not going to be eaten?" he said as he looked down at Jack and focused on his trusting, loving eyes returning his gaze.

"We are truth. What do you intend?" the warrior asked abruptly.

"John, I am seeking a new home for Jack and me, that's all. I'm just looking for peace."

"We are peace. I must know you, for there are human animals who have given up in the world, and there is no shame; they see no evil and yet use evil to survive another day."

"I understand, John. Please take me at my word. I have been raised well and believe in good."

"We have nothing for those who do not know the difference. Even after being told, they do not hear; they refuse to hear," the warrior said. Jeremiah easily believed his words.

Black clouds rolled in and began to block out the sun. A rain, sometimes dangerous, was about to fall. John motioned for Jeremiah to follow him and had a large, framed warrior drag his litter. Jack was hobbling along with them instead of being strapped down. Jeremiah turned toward the dog to make sure he could manage, but he doubted Jack could follow them a long distance without pain.

He moved toward Jack to pick him up in his arms, but John stopped him. He assigned another strong warrior to carry the dog. "Do not worry about him, Jeremiah," he said, smiling at the man who obviously was what he said he was.

"We'll be in the village in two hours, Jeremiah. You can rest there, and both of you will eat and drink. We will help the dog."

"Thank you, John. I'll do work for your village to repay the fare."

"We will not talk of such now, Jeremiah. Let us go and sit with the elders."

The clouds moved over them, and lightning strikes in the distance illuminated the background in wide streaks before the rain came. Jack followed him closely. The dog was frightened by the thunder and stayed as close to Jeremiah as he could while using his three legs to hobble along with his master and the group of warriors.

Soon, they walked into the village. Jeremiah noticed the cabins were nearly covered with vines and other green growth. At the center of the village was a large brick and mortar outdoor fireplace with a concrete floor—something used for cooking large portions. Stacks of wood to its north and south fueled the giant oven and open pit cooker. Each cabin was outfitted with a porch, and above the front door was a symbol whose meaning he didn't know. Further down the southern slope of the mountain they settled was a larger structure—the lodge used for group meetings, worship, and entertainment. Jeremiah and Jack were led to the lodge, where both of them were invited inside.

"It's here, Jeremiah, where the elders will meet you," John said.

He and Jack followed John's lead and took a place inside to wait. *These people are making a new life,* he thought. Suddenly, an entourage briskly entered and greeted Jeremiah and Jack. The elders were each dressed in traditional American Indian garb, some with headdresses, while others wore old baseball caps, and the standing warriors were uncovered from their waists to their shoulders. Jeremiah had thought there were no such people anymore—that they had been destroyed long ago and relegated to the pages of history, part of man's sorry legacy. They were a people who settled in North America before man nearly destroyed himself out of greed and hatred, where killing each other had become as easy as breathing.

"I am Stars Light, one of the people," the elder closest to him said as he extended his hand. Jeremiah took it and felt the strong grip the older man offered. He tucked his head down slightly in respect and humility.

"I'm Jeremiah. This is Jack."

"It's good that you have come to our nation. The evil world has become a horror, and good people must make their own way. You have shown John much, and so you are welcome here."

Food was brought into the lodge by several women and set out on the long table that centered the building. Jeremiah saw that there was bread, bowls of various greens, and cooked grain. The largest plate held slices of thoroughly cooked pork. Its aroma was one that Jeremiah remembered from long ago. It all came back to him quickly as the elders and warriors sat with them to eat. He noticed an unusual, curious thing on each face—a smile.

This is how it is supposed to be for people. We have lost so much, he thought.

Chapter 3

He noticed the beauty of the woman helping set the table. Although a natural sense for a man, he knew to keep his thoughts about them to himself. The long black hair was perfectly clean, straight, and flowing, much like an adornment of art but belonging to an individual as part of that individual. Jeremiah wanted to touch. To feel the grace he saw would be a wonderful thing. He knew that if he did, he would be touching beauty.

Stars Light handed him a cup. "Drink this, Jeremiah," he said, smiling.

The sweet and strong concoction was unlike anything he had ever taken before. It had a kind of clean though pungent aroma. He felt the swill traveling down his gullet and experienced a sense of well-being soon.

"Not for the dog," Stars Light said as he turned a cup up himself. "It is not good for him."

Jeremiah and Jack were taken to a cabin where they could rest and sleep the night on full stomachs. Different members of the warrior tribe brought Jeremiah and Jack blankets and water to make them comfortable. The mountain people, who had no pretense or greed, welcomed peaceful visitors. Jeremiah quickly thought he'd found a home.

The people of the mountains do not feel a need to kill for the sake of land or other material things. They could and would kill to defend their families and homes. Their life was one of existence in faith, hope, and peace above all, and they would risk their lives to preserve this way.

Toward the blackened cold north, near where once a city named Baltimore sprawled across the land and choked the waters, the leader of a people was speaking. The place now deserves the name taken from its leader's inspiration, Baal, and could have done so without reservation and still been accurate. The city ruler hated any reference to religion and what he considered myth and old fairy tales, including the existence of Satan. He named the post-war place as it was to him.

His adopted name, taken from bits of history, was Ostam, and a violent society was growing around the ideas he brought from his education before the days of the great light and fire. He wanted more power and land. Ostam's court had advised him that more food and fuel must be acquired before the next winter season.

"We must set a team to explore the reaches! It is time once again, for the sake of our people!" he said loudly to a congregation of over one hundred lieutenants and a few captains. "We have done what we could across the lands near and must find more. We've taken our resources as far as we can. We must go out soon and find the food and goods we need that can be used for the good of our people."

"We are with you!" an answer came back to him. The unison of one hundred voices committing to the challenge had become the expected. Over the course of several years, punishment by death within the people had become routine for offenses ranging from murder to dissent. No one dissented from the central command without facing such consequences. Their voices had to be silenced forever lest they corrupt the work for the good of all. He sent out armies of foragers once a year and was even now thinking about changing the schedule to a more ambitious foraging plan to bring in more.

"I want three teams. One shall go west, one to the south, and the third to our southwest," Ostam said, gazing at his crowd of followers who watched him with piercing affection. "You shall be given adequate supplies and arms to follow your hearts and take what the people need for their futures. You know what you must find. You know what you must do. There shall be no hesitation to do away with anyone or anything that tries to get in your way. Failure is not an option for those who are chosen for this work! Do not return except with good news!"

The list and agenda were long and extensive: fuel, food, weapons, equipment for land, housing, and people. The enslaved would include knowledgeable individuals in the sciences and engineering fields, constructors—and expendable others—workers who could labor and serve the most good for the survivor people—all must be found over the course of one year. Ostam's vision required much as he set about to rebuild a large and strong civilization of his dreams. He would head it all, become invincible and wealthy beyond anyone left in the burned world. He would be the most powerful and use his own wisdom to decide all issues and questions on a larger scale.

"You'll take one month. The ends shall be as I've laid out for you. Your mission shall not fail," Ostam said. His people knew what the words meant. Each team had to acquire all the wealth, fuel, fertile land, and if they did not fulfill the promise, their end would come without counsel, without a trial, quickly, painfully.

He chose a strong leader named Raymond to lead the team to survey south. Harris, an ambitious lieutenant, would head the group going west, and Morford, an older captain, selected the men and women for the southwest team.

Eighty-eight left with Raymond and began their southerly trek. A similar number of people went west, and a third army traveled south by southwest. The streams of sick, murderous impulses left the land of the people, human-formed tentacles stretching out toward their destiny of conquest. Each was led by a man with the same dispassionate and callous value for life, honed by years of their special education in the confines of the people's oasis of the Baal form of safety.

Ostam called for celebration and the cooking of many different farmed mammals to feed his people. He had his court, men who were with him after the day of light and helped him take power over all those who were left still serving as enablers. Gack and Sands were near the seat of power and had several unders bring out the heavy barrels of liquor for the higher class to enjoy with their meat while his band played their set over and again until the party was over. When he retired, everyone of privilege had their fill of the mind-numbing drink, the effects of which were akin simultaneously to alcohol and opiates.

The unders served at his pleasure until he tired of them, when they were sacrificed to save even the worst foodstuffs for other unders who were still able to work to his satisfaction. They came from lands that were close, far, or away, were of different colors, and some spoke different languages, and could never be accepted into Ostam's people. Ostam allowed them to reproduce, but for his purpose, only one child per female under was permitted. Any above that was snuffed out quickly. Pigs and several of the large dogs had to eat too. Unders deemed no longer fit to work were killed to provide protein for the animals.

An elder member of the court, Gack, kept track of each under's capabilities while Sands directed the guard to eliminate any of them who were no longer useful.

Jeremiah saw her in the hazy light of the morning. She brought him and Jack water and bread and gently placed the fare close to each visitor. Her long straight hair graced her shoulders and breasts, naturally covering its portion with a sheen and beauty he had rarely seen in his life. She softly told them it was theirs to use for strength for the day as she smiled. He swallowed her smile. He glanced back and forth between her and away from her to avoid being unseemly. She was a beautiful woman, though, and it was hard for him to divert his eyes for long.

He politely looked toward her feet and asked her, "What's your name?" He hoped she would answer him.

"I'm Katherine," she said through a kind smile.

"Katherine? You have a very beautiful name. How are you not out of place here?"

"I don't know what you mean, Jeremiah. Are you out of place here?"

"I'm sorry," he said. "I have only limited knowledge of the noble people of which you are a part."

"If you stay with us, I will gladly teach you our ways. We are a people guided by the spirit and believe in the Son who will return. We strive to remain prayerful and ever working until that day." She turned and left them.

What is this? I have heard such things before, in the long past. What can I give them in return for their kindness? I must find something, some way to repay these people. For it is keeping with what I have been taught, what I have learned back in time when my father and mother brought life to me. I am to give all I can and pay my own way.

Raymond and his small army were using the road Jeremiah had lived on for nine years. The vehicle in front was of old steel, protected by a layer of added armor plating. The last three trucks in the scavenger procession brought containers of fuel. Every four hundred miles, Raymond planned to leave one of the fuel trucks behind after its haul had been consumed. The plan would stretch them as far as the land formerly known as Florida if needed. His drive and thought were constants. He had to find all Ostam wanted before reaching the palms or face death.

As the army made its way into the land formerly known as Virginia, Raymond's point man stopped the convoy.

"Captain, we have travelers ahead… three hundred yards."

"Okay, watch for weapons. Invite them for water," Raymond ordered. "I'm coming up."

He and two of his guards ran to the lead truck. He saw there were three figures coming toward them. Through his binoculars, he could make out that there were two women and one man, covered with layers of clothing and each carrying a pack filled to its seams. When they saw the caravan, they tried to run away, but to no avail. Several soldiers jumped out of the fastest truck and quickly trapped them.

"Come on, come on," he said in a volume only he could hear. He turned toward his second-in-command, Lieutenant Richards, the point man. "Don't show your weapon! Let them come closer."

The three were within one hundred yards, marching along slowly, perhaps using every bit of strength they had left from their journey, whatever the proportions. "I want each of you to ready your machetes," Raymond said. "We won't have to waste bullets with this group. You there, stand ready with a rifle just in case," he said to one of his personal guards.

The man was the first to reach the truck and cautiously approached it as Raymond motioned for him and his group. "It's all right. We will not harm you. We have water for you," he called, loud enough for all of them to hear.

As his men brought out canteens and showed them to the group, Raymond noticed that one of them was older, a woman who looked to be in her fifties. She won't last long anyway, he thought as he smiled. The man was in his thirties and almost frail-looking from lack of nourishment. The second woman was younger and might be of service to his men. He would have to move fast to save her when his men began to do their job on the other two.

Suddenly the point man and his guards brought out their long chopping knives and sank the steel into the man's shoulder and through the top of his head. The older woman screamed as she took blows to her neck. Raymond tackled the younger woman and held her against the ground. He wanted her alive.

The man's head separated from his body with two precise blows. The woman's head was severed with one forceful strike. The job was done to Raymond's satisfaction. He smiled.

The young woman was crying, heaving, until she cried dry tears, and until her stomach was empty and convulsing. Her face and chest were shaking uncontrollably as Raymond forced her to stand. Her legs crumpled beneath her.

"Take her to the back of the second truck. Give her a little water and a slice of bread when she's ready to eat," the Captain ordered his Lieutenant.

Each body was thoroughly searched and stripped of all things of value—weapons, tools, maps, footwear, clothing—anything that could be used. The prize was fair. Raymond was able to collect a couple of blankets, a long knife and sheath, a cooking kit, and one pair of boots that were in good condition. The bodies were left where they fell as the convoy departed. Large wheels crushed the soft tissue into the asphalt; the crimson, stained, grayish-white waste and bone fragments spread on the surface much like the spill of a nightmare. Raymond never broke a sweat.

The woman was loaded into the back of the third truck where she was tied to the railings by her wrists and feet.

"Take us straight down this road," Captain Raymond commanded the point driver. We're off to a good start, he thought.

The convoy was within two hundred miles of the village where Jeremiah and Jack were learning about this new society. The convoy of evil men was bearing ever closer to their mountain.

Chapter 4

Stars Light, the wise, was one of the village elders and leaders when leadership was needed for safety, food, and good decisions. When the people's business required a final arbiter, he assessed the facts and gave a decision. He had grown wise and knowledgeable about life by listening to those who lived longer than he did. He strived to understand everyone and live in the spirit. He was responsible for determining whether Jeremiah was a threat to the tribe.

He thought Jeremiah was good, in the light, and had been taught well by his parents. He believed the young man could be one of the few left who had a conscience in this new world. He watched his care and affection for Jack. He saw his thankfulness for the food and bed—the modest way he accepted his portions. He observed Jeremiah treating everyone with respect. Stars Light saw all of this from the stranger and quickly formed his opinion of Jeremiah.

"You can have life here, Jeremiah," he said, pausing as he watched him. "If you wish, you can become part of this body and make your way with us, the people of the mountain," the old man said.

"I haven't paid you, Stars Light. I will make it right for all here and do work for the village which… you have given me so much," he said, his eyes filling. He felt more hope than he had known since he lost his mother and father.

"If that is what is in your heart, then let it be so. We do not make any demands."

Jeremiah lowered his head before rising to leave the lodge and seek out the labor he could perform. He thought he had left Jack behind but noticed the dog was next to him, walking on three legs, with every fourth step placing his left front leg gently on the ground. Jack didn't complain. His wagging tail signaled he was happy.

Several men were working with firewood, and Jeremiah was drawn to join them. He walked near them without saying a word and began to lift and carry sections of logs toward the two men who were the splitters. One of them was John, the leader of the warrior guards who found him. Others, including Victor and Katherine, were posted that day on the third mountaintop as watchers.

Beyond the cabins lay a field rich with growth. The village grew its own beans, carrots, corn, and an assortment of other foods. Jeremiah couldn't see the whole farm from where he chose to work. The field appeared to take up a large portion of the next valley in a wide swath of smooth layers of color.

"Jeremiah," came a gentle voice from behind him as he felt a hand on his shoulder. He turned to see Stars Light. "Struggle is patience. It is patience in all things. Struggle is the long way, the holding on to what you believe no matter what comes your way or blocks your path. The rock that blocks your way today only keeps you from stepping aside from it for a little while."

The newcomer noticed the old man's eyes, fixed and loving. Jeremiah thought he saw the soul of his heart, heard the music from his spirit, and was humbled by his words. He was in a hurry to prove himself worthy, productive, a contributor to the village. The younger man knew he had a great deal to learn and that he could learn in this place.

"I see you rushing to prove your worth," the elder said.

"Thank you, Stars Light," he said as he looked at the man's feet. "I am rushing. How do you know?"

"I can see the nervousness in your hands and feet. I can read your heart through the ripples dancing across your skin. Be not afraid, Jeremiah. You are welcome here. We say what we mean."

"I do want to be a better person, a good person."

"You are a good person. As we all begin, you were taught the important lessons from those who raised you until the day came when they could do no more. Your parents honored you, set in place a strong foundation, and you have honored them."

Jeremiah threw an eighty-pound log up to his shoulder and carried the weight to the split blocks. He glanced back at Stars Light. Katherine walked up to the old man and stood next to him to report what she saw while watching.

"There are trucks I can hear on the road," she said. "Many are on the road and have stopped where they noticed growth on the first mountainside. I fear it may be they who have come as foretold."

"Thank you, Katherine," he said simply to set aside her worry. That which was foretold was an expected story of a raid by outsiders that could change the life of the village forever—unless it was overcome. The old prophecy didn't include a specific day. It was inevitable though.

The elder called a council meeting for all the people. The lodge filled with anxious individuals within minutes. Men, women, and children gathered to hear the news, to learn what each was to do in the event the strangers came into their home.

"There are many strangers near our mountain," the elder began. "We cannot be certain they mean harm but we must be watchful. If their intentions are dishonorable, we shall have to fight them. If their intentions are honorable, we shall see to their needs and leave them in peace so that they may continue on their journey. We are sending thirty-three warriors out to track them."

She glanced in my direction, Jeremiah thought he noticed Katherine's eyes fix on him, causing his eyes to return the favor for a sweet second. If she was in his future, he never expected such a future. Nor did he think he would be part of a town or any group. Jeremiah was a solitary man with his dog, who made his own way, provided for his own, and let others be in the new world as it was. She was compelling. The people of the village were compelling. He clutched the sides of his head with his palms and pressed hard, rubbing back and forth to relieve the sudden pain. It is okay, then. What will come will come, and if it is to be this fond dream, then I surely want to submit to love. Should I be so honored to receive such a gift, then how can I throw it aside? What would my father do? What would my father think about me now? Could this be what he meant when he told me that I should always keep an open heart, a strong spirit, sure feet, and gentle hands?

"John, please let me accompany you and the thirty-three warriors to observe the others who are in our place," Stars Light said. He asked the people who would go with them. Jeremiah was one of the many who responded affirmatively. "We cannot all descend the mountain and go to the other," the elder said. "I'm sorry, but our numbers must be lower to avoid giving our presence away until we are ready."

Jeremiah had to be one of those selected. It could be dangerous out there with these strangers—and it probably would be, he thought. Stars Light and his village may not be aware of how the world has changed— and how bad it has become around the lands they lived.

"Please, Stars Light, allow me to be one of the chosen," he said, his head bowed, his right hand held firm and steady over his holstered .44. "Chances are these people want to take food from any source."

Ostam took the message from the runner who had traveled most of the night to reach the city. Raymond dispatched the young man with a note detailing his discovery of new growth and a seemingly rich mountain. Unlike most areas, there were trees sprouting here, along with bushes, grasses, insects, and a few animals spotted as they ran away from the noise. There was surely a water source nearby—a good start for a new land.

While waiting for an answer from Ostam, the convoy parked alongside the road. Jeremiah's former shack had been found and ravaged less than ten miles from where Raymond set up camp on the road. So far, the Captain's mission was going well. He envisioned being hailed as a heroic explorer, a leader of conquest on behalf of the power. Unders could cultivate the mountainside and its valleys. If the area was all he thought it could be, he saw himself as the master of the new city because he discovered it. Ostam would surely reward him with such a post. Raymond smiled.

"He should return with the answer tonight," he said to his Lieutenant and the closest guards. "Get a cooking fire going, and we'll eat today! I expect good news!"

At the same time, Stars Light and John were leading the thirty-three away from the village. Jeremiah was accepted as one of the warriors under the admonition to follow John and make no move, cause no sound. John was to show him the way.

The village warriors climbed and walked to the mountaintop overlooking the road. Many of their number could detect an ever-slight odor of the strangers through the occasional breeze that flowed up the mountainside and over its top. It was a mix of fire smoke, human sweat, and meat. They were close now.

"Move closer to see them, Wolf," John said to his son, one of the warriors. Little Wolf had long ago established his ability to be stealthy and unseen, even though he was only sixteen years old. He knew how to camouflage his entire body and cover his face to blend into the background of most areas. "We must know what you see, son. Be as unseen as the earth under your feet, become part of the land around you, and do not take an unwise chance."

The small young man prepared his body and began his approach toward the road. As he neared the strangers, the odors became stronger. Part of the smell made him think he might retch, but he had to hold it inside. Not a sound could be made. He crawled closer. Not a single bit of movement different from what the intermittent breeze caused the grasses could be made. His timing had to be perfect as he inched closer. Little Wolf came within fifty yards of the vehicle and remained in place, peering above the stones and grasses that hid him for any signs of movement as he strained to hear any words of the strangers.

He heard some of them speaking but couldn't make out the words. He had to get closer, but there was no more cover between his location and the road. The land was barren. He was part of the first patches of growth from the road that had been used over the years by a series of travelers in their search for food. The only chance he had to remain undetected and get closer to these dangerous-looking strangers was to wait until night—and hope the moon glow was dim. A snake coiled to strike inside a semi-circle of rocks and small stones within a few feet. It had sensed Little Wolf's presence.

Little Wolf heard the faint rattle and knew exactly what it meant. Sweat ran down his youthful face. He was losing water at a faster pace than he remembered ever losing before. The night was still hours away. There was nothing he could do until then but remain silent, one with the earth. He knew the direction where the serpent lay and how close it was to him, his face, and limbs—wherever he could be struck. Little Wolf thought he might back out of the area for a while and approach the road a little further north. He knew that strategy would be dangerous; every time he moved, he risked being detected by perhaps an even more dangerous life of these men. He considered moving but quickly dismissed the idea. His village depended on him doing the job at hand. He suddenly felt the first searing punch on the back of his right leg and felt the pain as the venom surged in a wave of burning rush traveling toward his hip. He didn't make a sound as he clenched his teeth, waiting for the next strike.

He focused on the beauty of his village, his father, and the people. He thought of the meadows and the crops, the dancing in the lodge, the girls he admired, the coolness of the clean waters, and the colorful beauty of their mountains. He felt the second strike followed quickly by a third. He had now been struck by the pit viper three times. He hoped the snake had had enough and would leave him as he felt sicker and sicker with every passing minute. He knew it might be only a matter of time before he would be unable to move.

The runner was expected to return with Ostam's answer before nightfall. Raymond simply needed affirmation. He knew that Ostam would populate areas closest to his fortress first, following the example of old Rome when an empire was built on the bodies of those who resisted closest to them. The armies he assembled were venturing further away from the center of civilization to conquer other lands.

Raymond was educated. He knew that every empire that fancied its own way to be the center of civilization had done the same throughout history again—and again, a constant—one people after another, one land after another. He understood this to be a necessary drive, a required work of superior human beings like Ostam's. He knew the same work had led to days of fighting and fire, but it was another new day, another chance to do it all and succeed for all time. Ostam was the leader who was convinced of himself; he believed he had learned from the mistakes of the past and was of a mind to kill in sufficient numbers to avoid another on the continuous line of downfalls of "great societies."

"This is it, then. He should return here soon," the Captain said to the guards and soldiers in his troop. "I want you all to check your weapons and be ready with plenty of ammunition. We will take the mountainside by foot and scope out what we have up there. You all will form a line. We'll advance shoulder to shoulder about twenty feet apart. Do not screw up! Don't fall behind the line or you're dead," he loudly warned.

Little Wolf heard enough to make out that the strangers were going to head toward their mountain. He turned slightly to begin the journey to the mountaintop, back to Stars Light, and started to back out of the place he shared with the snake. The serpent was gone now. He felt a swimming sensation beginning inside his body, interfering with his thoughts. His head left him dizzy. He was nauseous as the thief of sickness coursed through his body, stealing his energy and robbing him of clear thought. He shook his head to find focus. He took a deep breath and pushed it against the inside of his skin and organs to retrieve enough strength. He strained his eyes to find a safe path before forcing his body to respond.

The sun was slowly moving through the reddish sky, tucking itself behind the western slope of the first foothills. Little Wolf moved his prone body backward, using his arms and legs pressed against the ground, crawling low enough to avoid detection. He had to hope no one on the road would see him. If even one stranger noticed something moving, he would come over to see what it was or who it was so close to their camp. He crawled for an hour and then more before he thought he was out of their line of sight. Little Wolf was able to stand and walk toward Stars Light and his father when he noticed distant lights approaching the strangers' camp.

The messenger from the truck convoy returned with approval from Ostam. Raymond planned the excursion into the mountains at first light. He told his small army to sleep and be ready to move out with him. "We'll advance into the slopes and kill anyone we find there," he said. "I want every one of you to take all your ammunition—leave none behind. Do I make myself clear on what we must do?"

One element Raymond did not expect to find in the uniquely green mountain area was fuel. He planned to leave two guards behind to protect the supply they had. Failure to protect it meant a very long walk home and the executions of many on Ostam's order. It would test his food supplies and his patience with anyone who failed him. He went inside the cab of the second truck, where he could stretch out and get as much rest before the invasion as possible.

Little Wolf came into the perimeter where the warriors waited and stumbled several times by the time John and Stars Light saw him.

"Did you lose your water, Little Wolf? Please, sit and let us refresh you."

"No, father… I have been struck by a viper and could not protect myself in the place where I watched," he said weakly. "Another truck has joined them.

They are planning to come here. I do not know when, but I heard them say they were coming. They want the water and places to grow food. I fear we are going to be attacked, father," the young man said as his eyes began to close convulsively, painfully. "And I saw them leading a woman who was bound. She looked like a prisoner."

"We must attend to your bite, son. I will have two braves return you to the village so that you may be healed," the elder said, not knowing his son had been struck several times. He called out for two men nearby. Jeremiah heard him and ran over to help. Little Wolf was fading, though, and now it came faster. Before he could be lifted, he breathed his last, releasing his spirit away from his body and his body away from family and friends.

Stars Light sat silently, taking in the pain of this loss and letting it work throughout his own spirit and body. He felt sicker than he had ever felt. It was a complete wrecking of the heart, a complete breakdown of the body. He couldn't move. He couldn't think. The son had given himself to acquire every bit of information needed to protect his people. Little Wolf had given his life to save others, an act that was both a sacrifice and a privilege on behalf of a worthy people by an even more worthy brave. Jeremiah saw Stars Light motionless, tears streaming from his eyes as he remained silent. The elder was in a trance, for the cost had been agonizing and too hard to understand.

This seems to be the way it always is for good people. Better people give all for the rest—for those left, Jeremiah thought as he looked on Little Wolf and cried for the young man. Like me, I am left. What am I made of? Would I do the same? Father, mother, by your beautiful spirits, please say that I would save another. God in heaven, please give me the courage that I would do the same when the time comes to me… that I would honor the people who are good, who know you. To be less, to do less, is to be but an existence, not a man, a breather of air and little more than that.

Chapter 5

"We must set our last line of defense one hundred yards this side of the camp. If we do not stop them there, we will lose our people, our home," Stars Light said. The worried stress showed on his face, ridges of skin forming on both sides of his mouth and running the length of his neck, gathering skin now because of the advance of years. "There are many of them, and they have weapons for killing. We must wait silently and ready our defense. I will approach the leader alone to know them so that we will know what we must do."

"Can't we stop them from a distance, Stars Light?" John asked. "I fear it will be too dangerous for you to show yourself to these people who come our way armed for war."

"John, if I should fall, then you must lead our warriors in battle," the elder said firmly. "I know you will not fail them. If they attack, take out as many as you can here with the circle and then fall back to the others lying in wait for the fight."

John lowered his head and stared at the grass and rock beneath his feet. There was no arguing the point with Stars Light. He would go the way of Little Wolf if destiny took him there. The elder had one last statement to make, and that was to the guest of the village, Jeremiah.

"This is not yours to do, young man. Do not feel that you must stay for any time—or do any fighting that has come our way."

Jeremiah heard the words and knew he must do what is right. "I know you say it's not mine, Stars Light. Please, sir, this is where I am to be, and if it comes to a fight for the village, how can I walk away?" he said humbly. "May I speak more?"

"Very well, Jeremiah. What is it?"

"I want you to consider what John has said and let us call out from a distance. I can call out to you loud enough and still be hidden. We need you to stay with us. The village needs you, sir."

"That will not be, Jeremiah. I am in grave sorrow. My spirit is bruised deeply. I know what I must do for the village. Say no more. Leave me now and join John so that he may have as many braves ready to do according to his will," the elder said as he looked into Jeremiah's eyes. They both knew what would happen.

Pretending there was an even chance for peace was not realistic, and they knew that. The world was a place of others taking for themselves. It was a place of death. It always has been. Their mountains were now a place of the long past and even before, before people organized and claimed to be civilized but were not. There have always been killers and takers. The world was now the worst kind of nightmare for all of humankind, where life itself held no value. The village was one exception, and although the village people knew that there might be others, no one outside knew of them. The distance may be great. The waters of doubt may be impassable to rescue them all.

"Yes, sir, I'll join John. Thank you for allowing me to know you, and I hope that I may know you after these strangers are gone," Jeremiah plaintively whispered, for he knew that was not likely. He turned and looked toward the majesty of the trees behind them, subtly illuminated by the dim light from a rising red moon. He felt strong and talked to himself. Be strong, Jeremiah! Be on target and don't waste a single shell.

The warriors knew first light would likely signal the start of the advance. John positioned his thirty-one braves, including Jeremiah, in a semi-circle overlooking the closest and most likely trail that the army below would use to make their advance. Once Stars Light established their intention, the warriors would take action and deliver the answer the strangers deserved. What they would receive depended on them.

In Baal, Ostam summoned her to him. A female under named Mary had given birth to her second child, violating the law for the unders. Though human drive was as strong among the unders as it was among

Ostam's people, they were not to engage in any activity that could produce more than one child. For the unders, there were consequences for such a violation, easily enforced by the people. "You have had another under child?" he asked her in a smarmy voice. "That's number two for you, so you must turn it over to our store professionals."

"Please, Master, do not take my baby," she cried.

He heard her plea and was annoyed. He turned toward his Captain of the guard. "Attend to this under, Captain, and retrieve the evidence."

With a salute, the Captain took Mary by the arm and forced her to lead him to the makeshift shanty where her family lived in the large ghetto. It was the area where servants were forced to live until they died or were put to death. The man of the under family stepped forward to block the Captain's entrance, knowing it meant immediate death for him for such a daring action against Ostam's army. It was that inevitable moment when he had no choice. Knowing the outcome would be the same regardless, the husband—the father—stepped up—no words, no hesitation, just action. The Captain's second guard struck him down with one blow of a large sword to conserve precious rifle ammunition.

Now the pigs would have a larger carcass along with the newborn body to feast on. The adult male under felt no pain as he was quickly killed by the large blade that forcefully struck the top of his skull. The female child was alive when the Captain threw her into the fence-encircled mud.

The Captain was known as Dobey, no other name. Dobey was one of the most feared names in Baltimore, equal in viciousness only to Ostam himself. At the instant he released his grip on the baby's legs, finishing the motion of throwing her over, he was marked and could never know by whom. He would feel it. He could never understand why. The stain was inside him and set to grow from within until it consumed him.

On the road, two soldiers took the numbed woman and drove north, presenting her in the grand "house of the people"—the place that had once been a luxury hotel. The massive lobby provided Ostam the best platform he could find to dictate to his followers. "His name is James," she whispered mournfully into the air, knowing the child was at that moment being savagely torn to pieces. She felt their grip on her arms as she was being dragged away by Ostam's soldiers. She knew that no one was listening to her or cared about her.

"God, where are you?" Mary quietly mumbled, her tears soaking the entire front of the torn, crumpled, and stretched work blouse she wore. The loose fabric wrapped toward her left side as one of the guards held the back of it tightly to restrain her. Where are you, God? I have wanted to love you and be close to you, but it is much harder now, she thought in prayer. How can you let this happen?

"Can you not leave me where my husband and child died?" she managed to say with the tortured voice of a soul in agony, her heart wretched and torn as the baby was ripped from her arms. In that single instant, her life was over as she knew it. Though she had lived as a relatively unharmed woman for twenty years, she now understood that her place was to live as an under. Her place was to witness her baby's murder. She no longer wanted to live.

She remembered answering the first question when she and most of her close family, who survived the heat and light, came to this place searching for food. The question was whether she believed in God, and because she said yes, she was placed in the same class as all those who had answered similarly. She was assigned the under status of the new world ten years ago. Her name was Mary.

"You must come to justice. Ostam will tell us what to do with you," the Captain scolded. "He may want you to join your insolent husband and illegal baby with the cursed swine," he said through a laugh that sounded like a demon. "I'll not waste another word on you, under. I'll take your other child too and give him to Gack for your insolence."

On the road, Captain Raymond watched as the old sun began to light the landscape with a sheer touch quietly coming through the distance. It was still dark enough that a man could not make out objects or people more than a hundred yards away. He had his soldiers lined up and ready to move out at dawn, following the point man, a sturdy but less intelligent member of the people's army. The soldier was Private James, who happily took the order to lead the troop toward the top of the mountain so that Raymond could see all that awaited them on the other side and find the water source.

Stars Light watched those below form up and start the trek toward him. He looked up to the heavens and silently prayed as his ancestors had before every battle. His gaze returned to the line of strangers making their quick approach. He had minutes left to breathe, gather his strength, think of Little Wolf, and take comfort in the thought that if his spirit must be loosed this day—he had lived in the way his ancestors welcomed and Little Wolf expected. "Stay until you hear me, John. Take heart and be of courage, young man," he said. "You and the others have been taught, and so now, if I should fall today, it is you who will carry on the traditions and teachings of the people. As Little Wolf walked the path, I too will follow my son on the walk of life." With that, the elder rose from his knees and began to make his way toward Private James.

The snake of eighty armed men from the north climbed the slope, ready to kill. The point man moved as fast as he could toward the summit, excitedly trampling through new growth unlike anything he had seen before. The mountain was rich, and even he knew that meant good things for him and Ostam. Precious water and food, enough to last him a lifetime, waited ahead for him. He figured that if he was lucky, he could bring his woman to this place and live happily as a supervisor for Ostam. This journey and conquest were a crucial step that would make it all possible. I'll have a good future as a leader of the people for doing this job, he thought.

Private James pulled an exposed root to lift himself up a small ridge that suddenly appeared in the path, slowing their ascent. He quickly got over the ridge and saw the first glimpse of something or someone moving ahead. He stopped and squatted, signaling the closest soldier behind him to stop.

"What is it, Private?" Raymond called out, unconcerned about secrecy or quiet. "Report, damn it!"

"I think someone is just ahead of us, Captain."

"So, take us up, Private… do not stop. Find that under now!" he commanded.

Private James stood up on command and ran as fast as he could toward the movement. He did not have to go far as Stars Light met him straight on, standing directly in front of the stranger within moments. He stood erect and silent. The elder watched as the stranger raised the rifle he carried and pointed it directly at his heart. Private James had never seen another man dressed in such a way and wearing a dark feather in his hair —a sight that startled him at first glance. At second glance, the Private saw he didn't appear to be armed, which made the encounter seem fair in his mind. He kept the rifle trained on the odd-looking under's body mass and wrapped his fingers around the trigger.

"Who are you and why are you traveling this mountain?" Stars Light said.

Private James did not answer the under. Instead, he shouted down the slope to Captain Raymond while keeping his rifle aimed at Stars Light.

"Don't shoot yet, Private," Raymond shouted. "I want him to tell me what's ahead." The Captain passed his line of soldiers and quickly made his way to James and the person who was to be just another under.

Raymond saw the stoic figure just ahead, his unflinching chiseled face and eyes piercing the air between him and the strange presence that blocked his army's way. He must be a fool to come to us like this, the Captain thought. Maybe he's insane and alone in this rich garden.

"I'm Raymond. Who are you?"

"I am Stars Light. For what purpose do you come to my mountains? You are prepared for war. Are you here to make war?"

"Are you alone, old man?" Raymond asked.

"What do you want from my mountains?" The elder looked into the man's black eyes standing before him and saw no soul. "You're here for conquest," he said, his voice steady, deep, unflinching in the face of a murderous enemy.

Captain Raymond raised the rifle he carried and aimed it directly at Stars Light's chest. "I see green here, and we need that and water." He pulled the trigger and shot the elder once in the side, doubling him over and causing him to stumble. He did not fall. He stood straight again and said, "You shall not pass. Leave this mountain." He placed his left hand over the wound that was painful now, but he put aside the pain. He could not stop the bleeding, though, and crimson flowed down his skin to his left foot, covering his leather boot. "Now you tell me how many of you are up there!" Raymond commanded. "If you don't, you die!" Stars Light knew he was to die anyway and didn't utter a word. He stared into Raymond's eyes and did not blink.

John heard the shot. Jeremiah heard the shot. Victor, one of the warriors on the perimeter, knew what the sound meant and turned his head down. Every warrior heard the shot. Stars Light had taken the first bullet for the people, in honor of his son, and to protect their home.

Then a second shot broke the quiet once more on the mountainside, and they knew the man was dead. He had joined Little Wolf. It was up to them to stop the strangers now.

"Private James... go on up and don't stop," the Captain commanded.

Above them on the slopes, warriors were hiding behind stumps, logs, small trees, and rock formations. Each man dried his eyes. Those eyes quickly focused on the task of survival, of freedom.

John leaned toward the warrior closest to his position and told Jeremiah to pass the word. "Wait until they're near us. Make every shot count. Take good aim."

As he saw Private James, to him a murderous stranger and nothing more, Jeremiah rested his right arm across a small limb to take steady aim. The intruder stepped on a dead branch that cracked loudly and kept climbing while eighty others of the snake closely followed in a single wave. Jeremiah waited.

His right eye was open and sharp. His left eye closed. He could smell the man as he watched him stepping on their part of the earth. It was as if the ground was already his. Private James came within feet of him, the distance one could see a single tear fall to the same ground before it disappeared into the earth.

Jeremiah was the first to fire. He brought the man down with one shot centered on his forehead, and one out of the eighty-eight was gone. Raymond quickly ordered his army to disperse to the left and right and form a line of attack. The semi-circle of warriors began picking their targets and dropping several at once. The rest of the snake prepared to back down the slope and were quickly out of sight for a time, firing back wildly, their shots singing over the heads of every warrior or in the gulf of space between them since the strangers could not see them.

"This cannot be!" Raymond began to order Lieutenant Richards, a man who had purchased his rank by paying Ostam in women—his own daughters who were spared from the fire by holding up inside a bunker in Washington. He had been on a trip from what was Washington D.C. to Baltimore to arrange funding for favored politicians of the time who would vote with the administration for anything the administration wanted. Most of the politicians were dead now.

Although older than all of the other soldiers heading south, he nonetheless held his position because Ostam appreciated his gifts. "I need to know how many there are up there and how far to each side is covered. We have to flank them and come down on them to kill every one of these disgusting unders. Get four men and take them north up the slope and find out what we have up there."

Lieutenant Richards stared toward the leader in fear. Captain Raymond saw that he was lost. The older man's gaze was past him and into the air. The man began saying something under his breath that Raymond could not clearly hear or understand, as he had no patience. His life depended on his mission.

"Get moving now, Lieutenant, or I will drop you right here, right now!" he said, his guttural voice making it clear to Richards that he was serious and would not hesitate. There was no political contact, friend, or indebted person alive, anywhere, who could save him this time. Raymond was the Captain of this land-bound ship of an army, and whatever he commanded was to be done without time to waste.

Although fear had him by the throat, the fear of Raymond brought him to his feet. The Lieutenant pointed to the five men who were lying closest to him and waved them to follow him. Without a word, he set out to the left along the ridge. A warrior picked off one of the soldiers as soon as they started to move. His head exploded, and the body fell limp to the ground. Richards began running as fast as he could negotiate the angle above his right foot and led the patrol further down the slope to escape the shots.

"Jeremiah… I need someone to follow that group. I fear they are trying to come around and on top of us."

"I'll do it, John," he said as he began to move toward his right and quickly follow the patrol they had seen only glimpses of and now had lost sight of in the crevices and angles of the mountainside. He would have to find them first and kill them all. He had to take them all, or many village warriors would be killed.

Jeremiah was not sure how many intruders were coming around to attack the village warriors from the rear. He saw a small bit of movement and was able to track them as the earth's growths gave way ever so slightly against the rushing bodies of Lieutenant Richards' troops. The new growth was helping him fight off the unwanted. He moved like a fast whisper through the trees and bushes, barely making a presence, closing in on his quarry at will, at the timing he saw best. He counted four of them close and didn't see more this far out from the rest. It was a challenge before him unlike any he had ever faced, even as he stopped one stranger after another who wanted Jack, scratched for survival, and consumed vomited berries along the trails. His shots had to each hit their mark. He had to stop all of them.

Lieutenant Richards was well away from the center of the battle. The three remaining soldiers waited behind him, crouched the same way he was, hiding from any sharpshooter.

"I think we're far enough to move up the slope and come in behind them and on their right. I need a volunteer to move up," he said. No one moved a finger, hand, or eyelid.

"I think you should go first, Lieutenant," the largest soldier said. The dry monotone of his voice threatened Richards.

Jeremiah saw the movement stop, so he waited, concealed by friendly plants and trees. His reflex was to hold the .44 toward the last man of the patrol where it may be resting. Lord above, let me see. Let me protect. Guide me, strengthen me, give me good aim, he prayed.

Jeremiah saw the first one begin his climb up the slope. He let him pass and watched for what the others would do. He was sure there were four of them as they climbed, making a wide circle. The second one moved low and stayed mostly concealed. He watched him as he scanned behind his trail for other movement. The third one was close behind him, and the last killer used some distance to separate himself from the other three.

Jeremiah noticed a draw to his left that would give him some cover, and he could use that to begin firing on the last one in line and then move to the other three. He eased down into the slight draw on the side of the mountain and caught the fourth man within twenty feet of his new position. Wasting no time, he leveled his pistol, fired into the man's chest, and quickly fired a second shot that took his head.

The recoil of the first shot aligned his pistol for an immediate second shot that would strike the head if the trigger was squeezed a second time in perfect timing. He shot the second round and watched it tear through the center of the marauder's head. The body fell as a mass against the earth. Jeremiah felt stronger in his arms, hands, and throughout his body than he could ever remember feeling. Nothing, no one, could stop him. He felt steeled and doubtless.

He began the climb to follow the others and did not stop until he had taken down the next one; in quick succession, the second intruder was put to waste by his gun. That left Richards, who had curled up in a ball behind a small rock when the firing started. The Lieutenant had soiled his clothes. His hands were shaking uncontrollably; his feet felt as if they were both on fire and weighed down with concrete. He couldn't see because of the sweat and tears. Jeremiah looked for his movement and, not seeing any, knew he had to go find him. Even a single armed invader behind his people could be disastrous. He was going to succeed. The wings of a thousand eagles and the strength of many bulls pulled him easily toward his objective. It wasn't a matter of whether he would find him but when and how soon he could return to the rest to defend against the main force attacking them.

Jeremiah crept up the slope to the last place he saw movement and waited. In the time it took him to draw two breaths, he heard something. That has to be my target. He heard sniffling and crying—fear expressed by a body unable to restrain itself from pouring out, no matter how hard Richards tried to stifle it. Jeremiah knew where the last man was hiding. He was over the rock in as short a time as possible and had Richards in his sights.

Without hesitation, he placed one bullet through the man's head and stopped all the sniffling. Jeremiah gathered the weapons these strangers brought and all the ammunition he could find on their bodies before he returned to John.

Raymond knew something more was involved with taking the green and water, and that his mission had taken a turn he didn't expect. The old dead Indian was not alone. The sound and sequence of the firing he heard were not from his soldiers. The bad sign of a long silence meant he had lost four more soldiers. He motioned for the army to withdraw with him back to the road. He could not know what was waiting on that mountain. He had no choice but to attack again because he knew that Ostam would surely execute him for failure.

Chapter 6

"This is the plan," Captain Raymond began, sweating more water out of his body than he had taken in. "We have to find a different way into that mountain range and discover what we are facing. Our job at this point is to get up there, find them on our terms, and kill them. That's our job. They must have food and water, and it belongs to our people."

The body of Stars Light was returned to the village. He was to be interred next to his son. The warriors gathered in the lodge to honor him first and mourn their loss. Katherine and the other women of the village brought water, oils, and towels to clean and anoint all the men's faces and their sore, tired feet. Some of them were bleeding from brushes with rocks and branches as they fought off the murderous strangers. Their work had just begun. There was little time to rest in the village. Every passing minute was causing Jeremiah to become more anxious about stopping the enemy.

He wiped his face with a towel and glanced around the large room. His darting eyes captured the makeup of the defense against the many. We need to get ready now, he thought as Jack came to him and began licking his face. If those people have their way, there will be no one left to survive, and they'll eat Jack and all we have here.

"John, how many warriors can we gather?" Jeremiah asked in a whisper to the strong man sitting next to him, in prayer for Stars Light.

There was no answer. Jeremiah knew he would have to adapt to more of the village culture than he had so far. Finally, John looked up.

"I'm sorry, John. I should have never spoken when I did. Please forgive me for the transgression against the honor of Stars Light."

"Do not think about it now or after this hour, Jeremiah. I am not offended. Stars Light knew you to be an honorable man, so he would not be offended either—more important than I."

"Thank you. I'm worried about the strangers. They'll kill us all if we don't stop them."

"You're right, but do not worry for us. We will turn them away."

"There are many of them, and they are well-armed," Jeremiah said.

"We have arms too, and now we have four more rifles thanks to you, along with ammunition to use in them. We'll do what we must do, Jeremiah. Thank you for what you did today. You are a proven warrior on your account now. I know we can rely on you in battle."

"I pray to live up to it and never fail these people."

John smiled at the newest member of the tribe. "You will, of that I am certain, Jeremiah. Now, we have little time to prepare and must begin. I shall keep the council and the people gathered. We will decide what to do within this night."

"I fear the strangers are moving under the cover of darkness, John. I'll go to watch for them."

"That has already been done."

"I would have remained behind to watch them, John."

"I know. You did great work today, and others will do what their hearts drive them to do as well."

"Of course," Jeremiah said. He was learning the ways of the people quickly. So much was coming onto him that he thought it was changing him, and that change was good. He could feel his own heart taking a better place as the true source that caused such want, a want that he had to let loose. True freedom was bursting out of him, demanding full expression.

"Ostam, great leader, what shall we do with the woman?" the Captain of the guard said. He showed Ostam the filthy, slovenly dressed woman kneeling, resting on one arm away from the marble floor of the leader's parlor for judgment.

The prisoner's head was tucked into her chest. She refused to look upon the cruel face of the man who had killed her family and so many others. The leader looked at her and saw a woman he could use.

"Have you taken care of the baby?"

"Yes, sir, and the husband was eliminated too. He tried to fight us when we came for her."

"Very well, Captain. Take her to Rachel. She'll know what to do with this insolent one. I will make her a prize for the first Captain to return with good news."

"They're using the southern cut toward the first valley; the strangers will be able to find the village within a few hours," a warrior said between hard, deep breaths he needed from the run.

"Very well, we'll meet them where the twin oaks are rooted." He turned to the council and the people of the village. "Gather your bands and have them leave for battle. We must remain on the high ground and stop them there."

The two hundred stepped out and took the mountain paths made long ago to intercept the strangers in the deadly duel that was to be destiny for all the people. Though many women wanted to join them, John asked that they remain in the village and take up arms around its perimeter in case the strangers broke through their line.

It was in the green, in the unbroken breeze of the valleys, near the trees of hope where the tribe went to meet the enemy. Men who gladly risked death to defend their home, their place in the new world, formed the lines. Jeremiah joined them with his .44 and one of the rifles he took from the strangers. Katherine gave him a bandana to cover his forehead. The green, blue, and brown cloth was hers and carried her scent closely. The village's numbers were superior, and Stars Light's fear of their intentions proved correct.

Raymond was moving his army quickly up a divide where they found safety because of the concealment the land offered. There was no sign of the village defenders yet as they made their way up, and Raymond was confident they would be successful on behalf of Ostam. He knew he was smarter than "these unders" and sensed an easy victory. A few hundred feet left, and they would be able to come down behind the unders who had taken so many of them earlier. The night was giving way to the sunrise. Raymond thought that he nearly had his men in position and would be able to surprise them below. Then he would take the mountain and the next one and own all of their riches. His mouth curled up at its corners before he spread his forces wide.

His smile revealed black and brown teeth, one of them pointed, another cut at an angle, and others missing. He could taste the fresh water. He could smell the cooked meats. He could see his kingdom filled with women of his choosing who would be forced to cater to his every desire and unders working to keep him ever comfortable, ever higher.

"Once we get to that point," Raymond said, his arm extended toward a cluster of trees as the mark, "take forty men to the right, Private. You take the rest to the left. I'll remain in the center as we come up on these unders," he said to the two guards closest to him.

John and the village waited. Their weapons were loaded and ready. Their eyes were set. A cluster of trees centered the wall of warriors.

Hundreds of eyes saw the murderous strangers coming toward them. They waited until the invaders came closer, until many of them were on the slope, close to their destiny. They came to meet that destiny delivered by a free people.

In an instant, the throng of warriors rose up and fired into the mass of men clustered together below them. The fire was a single sound of horror as blood sprayed and bones were pierced of many invaders. Many fell dead from the first volley. Others panicked and began to run, stumble, and fall down the slope. Among the frightened was Captain Raymond himself, who was trying to run away. He had no appetite for what he had led them into—a fight they were quickly losing.

John waved the braves to follow. Jeremiah jumped and ran toward the enemy, taking down the first one he found trying to escape with a well-aimed shot to the back of his head. Others followed suit and eliminated others as they rolled down the slopes, too slow to escape. Weapons and bodies crowded parts of the path. Blood ran down the slope. Flies and worms had a quick feast laid before them in large numbers by the accurate fire of village men.

"We must take to the trucks and find the woman!" John called out. "You twelve come with me please, and the rest of you form up around the village." He was preparing for a counter-attack if it came.

"I want to go to the trucks, John," Jeremiah spoke up, as was his habit. He followed John to the center trail, the quickest way down to the road. The thirteen ran to the trail and then ran down the slope.

"We can't be late! We must get there before them."

"How many are left, John?" Jeremiah shouted down to John between breaths.

"I don't know how many, friend."

We may be rushing into a trap much as we set for them, Jeremiah thought. He tried to pass John on the trail in case he was right so that he could be safer.

"What are you doing, Jeremiah?" John's breathless words were pushed out of his diaphragm.

"They could be waiting somewhere down below."

"I'll lead the people here! Please just stay ready. Have the eyes of an eagle. Use the cunning of the raccoon." John knew the man well now. He recognized him as a brave warrior among their blessed number.

They did not slow down as they broke into the open field between the mountain base and the road. The two guards rose up. After hearing the firing, the guards he left behind assumed that Captain Raymond had killed the protectors of the mountain. Jeremiah and John put several shots toward them, causing the two to dive under the second truck, their closest cover.

John was on them as soon as they were under the frame and ended their duty as guards before the two could beg for their lives or fire their weapons. He searched the back of the second truck as others searched the rest of the convoy until they found the bloodied woman. Quickly, a warrior untied her while a second one removed the gag in her mouth, a soiled rag the people of the north used to muffle her crying. The thirteen left the road for the mountain within minutes.

"Who are you? What are you going to do to me?" she cried out.

"We're the people of the American village, and we will not harm you! We're bringing you food and water," John said. "Do not worry. Your trial of this day is over."

Jeremiah overheard John use the word American and began to cry. He had not heard that word since his parents were alive. It was their prayers answered, their only dreams come true by the virtue of a small group of people who found refuge in the mountains.

"I'm in your debt," she said.

"We will be going into the mountain," he said. "If you're not strong enough to walk and climb, our people will carry you."

John took the twelve back through the same middle trail. There were fewer bodies to pass, and they made their way up the trail past where Jeremiah had found them. He did not want her to see more death. It sickened him too. Halfway up the grade, he turned and saw what appeared to be the leader and many others who came from the trucks. The day had just begun, and they had two mountains to cross and the slope of a third. It would take them many hours moving as quickly as they could.

Captain Raymond returned from the distance he had covered while running and began to set his defenses up in the line of trucks. He ordered his remaining men to remove the bodies of the two failed guards and cursed them for their failure. Somehow, part of this group—these unders—had stolen away from the battle, killed the guards, and taken the woman. He walked in fear, though. He knew the ghost-like humans he had to eliminate for the land could be watching him. Ostam would not understand. He wasn't the kind of man who accepted failure. His words came back to him that afternoon. You will take one month. You shall not fail.

It had only been a single week, and he had already lost thirty-six soldiers. The messenger had brought Ostam a message of conquest of a rich land as he was securing approval. This victory had to be won here, now, and finished no matter the cost.

Not having a choice to go further or turn back, it was on him to succeed against this stubborn foe. There has to be a way, Raymond thought. I can't ask him for more men and weapons. He would know something was wrong and will put me to death for the pigs.

John told his warriors that they were to cause the invaders to be without strength. "The way we do that is to keep them all on alert throughout the day and every hour of the night. They are still on the road and are right now planning to kill us. We'll work in shifts and fire on them from the foothills as we become part of the earth. The invaders cannot be allowed to rest, and if they remain, they must die."

Katherine learned the rescued woman's name was Sara. She began to clean and treat her wounds in the cabin built next to the lodge. In Katherine's care, Sara knew that all John said to her was true, and she cried. In the world as she had known it for so many years now, she had not experienced the music of kindness until this day, her most desperate day.

Chapter 7

Raymond had an unexpected challenge; this group of unders had to be put down and he had to do it quickly. There was no accurate intelligence as to what he was facing. It didn't matter. Ostam gave them no allowance. His armies were to find new, prosperous lands whether they faced armed enemies, whether in small or great numbers.

His choices were few. He would have to attack again as he did last time or approach from a different angle. He had to take the high ground again. If it meant losing every single man with him, he would do it to take this mountain. He would not share that with his army. He had to use them, and if that meant witnessing their deaths, he would do so without a second thought. Raymond himself would rather die quickly here than face Ostam and the pigs.

"We'll take a wider swath and move against these animals. We are going to tack one mile south and then move up the mountainside. We have to kill them all! Let's get to it," he said.

The marchers from Baltimore set out at a quick pace down the road until the trucks were well out of sight and the paths they had explored before were far behind them. Raymond would lead them this time to avoid a mistake by a less vigilant point man.

Some hundreds of miles away, Morford and his army were moving into what was once Texas. Harris had taken his trucks and army into the land formerly known as Illinois. Neither of these captains had encountered the kind of resistance Raymond faced. Each of the other armies had killed a few passersby they came across in the west and southwest.

Some of the poor, needy souls often approached the convoys, thinking there might be help and food for them. Their bodies were left where they fell to decompose in the open air. Human remains scattered across the land were no longer unusual. There was green and water ahead for both, but at a greater distance than Raymond's find. Even though the earth had begun to heal itself, recovery from the day of fire was a generation slower than the world had known. Its eventual health was very much in doubt, as new growth could wither and die any day nature was strangled by weather. Abandonment could have very well occurred in other places in other galaxies. No one on earth knew.

John took the message from the runner who had returned to the village from the first mountainside. Jeremiah watched as John's face transformed from sorrowful and reflective to something fierce. He knew the man was contemplating killing. Jeremiah saw his eyes pinched between dry eyelids, his chin firmly set, his mouth closed and drawn back, ready for battle.

"What is it, John?" he asked.

"They're coming again; this time they are moving on us from the south. They're not leaving us in peace, so we must destroy all of them. Let's leave now to meet them."

"I'll go ahead, John. You need to know exactly where they are, and I will find them."

"Very well, Jeremiah. The women will form a line with weapons behind us, and the rest of us will meet them as the first line. Don't be careless."

The war would be settled in its impending intersection of hardened hearts and heartless, soulless men. The people were prepared to use the necessary force to protect the village. It was the village or the intruders. Their decision was made, clear that it had to be this way. They came to kill, and so must be killed first if the village was to survive. They had to do the worst, the filthiest thing men can possibly do to other men.

The last thing John did before they set off was gather the village in the lodge and do his best to convey what Stars Light would have told them if he were addressing his beloved people. "I am not Stars Light, but

I must tell you what I know. We are at war and must defend our homes. The strangers are coming for us and will kill as many of us as they can, enslaving those left alive. It's a horror inflicted on our nation that must be stopped. I'm sorry, so very sorry, that we have come to this… now a deadly conflict is upon our people," he said, taking a long breath.

"If it could be any other way, then it would be. On this, you have my word. I cannot ask you to take up arms against another human being without it being an absolute," he said, thinking of Stars Light, envisioning him in his mind, listening to every word he would say. "As we must do this, we must be sure and resolved with all our spirit, making it as quick as possible by taking perfect shots. Stay out of their range and field of fire, use cover, and be like the earth—become mother earth, unseen, coiled with a viper's strike. Now, we face them. Follow me."

That night, the army led by Raymond was no more. As the smoke began to clear, several dozen bodies were revealed, along with all the gore that munitions can cause as they tear into human flesh laid out on the ground. Warriors issuing a final judgment, one last shot where needed, quickly silenced the screams of several who had not been killed outright. John's warriors considered the act a mercy for the unmerciful. There was a tainting of those patches of earth where each fell as their hearts beat for the final time.

The Americans did not lose a single man. It had been a slaughter unlike anything the village had known since the day of fire and light— this time by their own hands. Twelve warriors posted on the road removed the few intruders who escaped and ran back to the convoy. Each attacker took twenty or more shots to their bodies and fell lifeless in quick succession. There was no quarter given, no debate, no chance. John turned to the warriors. He saw one of the young ones, Victor, crying over what he had done. The terrible trap of necessity intersecting with killers bent on killing his family forced him to kill. The quiet warrior turned away from the carnage and began to make his way home.

"This will not end here. Wherever these came from, there will be more to follow to hunt us down. We must bury the bodies, then return to the village and tell everyone what we have done. We have killed many men. We must always bear the weight of dread for acts that are the most severe, be men of sorrow for our anger, and take responsibility for taking life—the thing that only God has the right to claim. Our dilemma is whether, by acting in God's name, we have done right or wrong. We pray it was right in His eyes."

The village worked quietly to return the dead strangers to the earth. There was no joy, no celebration for what they had done. The area was marked with a six-foot stack of stones. The weary warriors marched back to the village in silence.

"We should not return to that sacred slope… It's not a part of us; it is ageless," John said to the gathering of the people inside the lodge.

Sara listened even though she had yet to understand the people. Her strength had returned, and she was able to help Katherine with work. Sara cried over her mother and husband. Her tears came at unexpected times, with little or no provocation. Still, they flowed when they came and were beyond her control. The village would enjoy a needed week of peace.

Ostam heard from Morford about the southwestern second front within a week. There were acres and acres of new growth his army found and was establishing a permanent camp with the great leader's permission. He had led the convoy not even thirty miles into North Texas when they discovered it. Protected by its isolation, the fires had swept over it once but did not destroy the seeds just under the surface. There were saplings and much greenery, no one around to interfere, and relatively clean water.

Nothing was left of the inhabitants other than small piles of bones, almost in a concentric pattern as if they were deliberately piled up by others, who must be dead too. There were no bodies still holding flesh of the last survivors that he noticed, so Morford assumed the vast space was his and that his mission for Ostam had been accomplished.

Morford heard a sound in the distance and quickly turned toward it, where he saw a deer jumping and running away. Another good sign that this was the place, he thought. He dispatched two of his guards to hunt the animal down for their meal that night. He glanced back at one point and noticed them walking into the horizon, enveloped by the shimmering waves of heat rising from the surface. They soon became too far away to see. He relaxed in the cab of the lead truck while his men built shelters and a fire pit. He flipped his cap down over his brow as he felt the gentle breeze of the North Texas winds cooling the cab.

This had been an easy one. He reflected that he had managed far more difficult assignments from Ostam in the past and survived them. The occasion of the raid into what was Washington D.C. was the hardest because, though there were few left, the enemy had weapons and came bounding out of bunkers to stop him. He lost over fifty men that day and left their bodies in a pyre set just after taking the Capitol building. Much of the silver, gold, and fineries such as wall décor, desks, and chairs were unscathed in the day of fire, and he took much of it back to Baltimore. He smiled, proud of himself and content. He would be in line for promotion because of the rich earth he found and claimed for the people. This time was surely his. He didn't have the annoying job of burning any bodies either.

He envisioned women and luxury for himself. He saw the future down here in this place where he would rule. The power and all that came with it would be his, and no one would stand in his way. It was going to be absolute, and his word would be the final word. His will would be done in this new community.

Morford awakened after a sleep and stumbled out of the cab. "How long have I been asleep?" he asked the first guard he saw.

"About five hours, sir," the younger man replied.

"Where's our deer?"

"They haven't come back yet, sir."

"Get ten others and go find them. Bring them back here—and the deer too. I'm hungry."

The patrol set out in the direction the two soldiers were last seen chasing the deer. They too were soon out of sight as they followed the trail. Morford settled back inside the truck's cab and began drinking his wine.

The patrol was two miles away when it happened. The newly appointed corporal of the guard saw two bodies lying more like rags along a bare portion of the trail than the remains of human beings. The clumps of cloth and flesh had no effect on him, for he was accustomed to death, but he did not know what had happened to them. He closed in for a closer look while his men stood by, scratching their faces and chests. Each man felt as if something was crawling on his skin, ever so slowly but definitely, as if each had suddenly attracted the attention of large insects. The cause was not insects, as there was nothing they could see attaching to their bodies.

The Corporal studied the bodies, ignoring the itch he felt. It appeared to him as if they had been set on fire as he suddenly felt his own skin erupt with something he didn't understand. He did not know that his fate was already determined—it was too late for him and those he brought with him.

He clawed at his clothes and tried to put out an invisible flame that was engulfing him but could not. As he fell in pain unlike anything he had ever experienced before, he saw the carcass of the deer just ahead. He breathed his last though trying to avoid taking this air inside of his lungs. He wrenched and screamed with the others until finally, he and they were no more than clumps of refuse in a circle of desert centered in greenery that covered the landscape. Only a half-mile near-perfect round was barren earth, except for skeletons and carcasses of those creatures and men who passed through the peculiar zone.

In Baal, Ostam had heard nothing from Raymond. He's gone against me, the bastard! I'll teach him a lesson and replace him while I bring him back and feed his traitorous hide to the pigs! How dare he take from me and keep it all to himself! He's going to try to set up his own city against me!

"I want Raymond found and brought back to me!" he shouted at the Captain of the guard, Dobey. "It's been too long without word! He's been on his own for over a week and still no word! Get him, now!"

"Yes, of course, sir, but he has over eighty men."

"Then you take two hundred and do not fail me! Kill them all if you have to, but I want him alive when you bring him to me. Leave the rest to rot where they fall! This is an outrage!" I'll show them all again who is in charge and what it means to disobey me! I have two more armies doing my bidding and they will bring me good news or meet the same fate, he thought. Ostam threw back another goblet of wine toward the back of his throat and finished it off with one swallow. He turned toward the gathering of women he kept as a constant convenience and quickly selected one to take back to his chambers. He left Captain Dobey to gather his forces and make his way to Georgia that night.

"Do not fail me, Dobey," the leader turned back and said.

"I will not, sir, for all that is in me is for you and our people. Raymond will be found and held to account for his negligence."

"See to it," the leader said as he turned back to the woman, taking her arm to walk her into his chambers.

Dobey went outside where his lieutenants had two hundred strong standing at attention, waiting for him—waiting for their orders. Unders who were assigned to vehicle maintenance had thirty cars ready to run, eleven pickup trucks, and six larger flatbed or covered trucks repaired enough and fueled at the Leader's or army's disposal. Dobey had all the armed men quickly form into the large convoy as he led it south, following the same route Raymond took weeks ago.

John, Jeremiah, and the village only had a couple of days before the large force of invaders would show. He asked Jeremiah to take a small work party, move the vehicles out of the roadway, and hide each of them. Jeremiah felt honored by the request.

"Thank you, John, for allowing me to join you," he said, his head turned down out of respect.

"Do not look down, Warrior Jeremiah. You're welcome as part of the people here. You're the same as me. We do not place anyone on a high plane, and it must remain so."

"I'll hurry, John. We do not know how far those who may come after them must travel."

"That's true, Jeremiah, nor do we know there will be some to follow. We cannot chance that there won't be more sent to ravage our lands. I pray there are not more to come, but our world has been altered by the evil one many times and never stops. I fear we have to fight him forever."

Two of the large trucks were towed behind others. Jeremiah was able to hook them together and pull them down into a ravine where he had every vehicle covered with dirt and materials that had been torn years ago. He tried to make it appear to be a pile of construction materials destroyed, as most were during the day of fire and light, but there was no way he could completely cover the evidence. He and his crew spent some of their time cleaning the road of body parts and the obvious bloodletting. The deep stains in the old asphalt and concrete would not go away, but he hoped it would not be noticed as anything that happened recently from other portions of the same road.

Jeremiah sensed it first. He felt the same foreboding he had many times in his life after the great fire. The same feeling invaded his heart many times since the days of the light. He turned and saw the darkness traveling toward their mountain. He felt the wind, a hard wind bringing it all. A storm was coming toward them quickly and would soon cover them.

These storms were different from the thunderstorms of the past. Now the lightning was an odd color, indescribable, still yellow but with a red border as if some unseen hand repainted it. The typical hail was gray in color, not white, and was no larger than the size of peas. The rain would often burn the skin if one was caught in a downpour unprotected. It often felt more like little pins of fire than droplets of wet he remembered from his boyhood.

"The storm will be on us soon. Take cover in the ravine well away from the steel," he called out to the few who were with him on the mission.

The warriors ran down into the slight depression and moved toward its end where the contour came out of the deep cut and onto level ground. There wasn't much cover as they huddled together against the edges of earth under a short growth of saplings and bushes as they waited for the storm to hit them. They gathered and threw up as much material from the shirts and leather coverings they wore as best they could to deflect the rain and hail. Quickly, the warriors had a makeshift lean-to to cover them.

Chapter 8

"I better hear good news," Ostam had declared to the next army he would punish should it be unsuccessful. "Find that Raymond quickly and bring him to me!"

Dobey led a newly formed army south, driven by Ostam's command. He was single-minded in purpose. It mattered not that the treacherous Captain Raymond was his brother, born of the same woman. Whatever he was doing outside the order had to be stopped and brought back to Ostam's Baltimore to pay the ultimate price—a date with hungry pigs in their wallow of half mud, half blood. The food source for Ostam's favored waited half-submerged in the dark reddish, near-liquefied home for their next meal.

Evil watched the procession of men leave the city from an upper floor of the columned building that once housed politicians. He was no politician, a form of humanity he knew of from the past and held in equal contempt, seen through the cold eyes of a soul long given over to darkness. His face was fixed in an expressionless, sour, violent scowl. He represented Satan as well as any man did before his time on earth. There had been countless contenders for the title of the most evil, dark, soulless, hate-filled—the worst concepts born when the world itself was created.

What he could not know was that he had brought his brand of evil to a peaceful people in the mountains, simply living in harmony with all that remained of a gravely ill earth. He could not know that the society he was attacking understood enough history to know and love liberty. He could not know the people he wanted to kill and steal from were filled with the spirit of the fight—the true God of love. The Indian tribe would die to protect that freedom, as many had before this generation. For the American warriors, there was no question or debate about the choice everyone must make, nor any doubt about the sacrifice required.

The storm had passed over them, and their cover had protected them all. Jeremiah was among the first to emerge and see what they had to deal with as they set about returning to their beloved home nearby, where the trees sheltered their families. The village of the American tribe worked to prepare a meal after the storm passed, and cook-fires were lit again. Katherine finished kneading dough for the bread and prepared loaves.

The path on the road and into the forest was washed away with such force that half of it was gone; deep ruts had been cut in the way, and some trees had fallen across it. Mud was more than a foot deep in places. Jeremiah began the journey home, trying to force his mind to remain solely on Katherine and finding warmth again. I don't know if our threat is actually gone or if it will come back on us tonight, he thought.

Jack greeted him, as he did every time Jeremiah returned from a day's work. The dog ran toward him happily, wagging his tail and whimpering to see his master, jumping up to get as close as he could to Jeremiah. In turn, he picked up Jack to hold him in a loving embrace. The human half of this loving partnership stroked his coat and bent down to kiss him on the side of his furry face. Jeremiah dodged the dog's tongue as fast as he could, but was rarely quick enough. Jack never failed to make Jeremiah smile. Seeing him brought a rare joy in these times.

Soon, he would need to set out and walk a wide perimeter to protect the village from any stranger who wanted to attack them. Soon, he would leave Katherine's presence again, carrying her aroma, appearance, and gentle ways in his memory for the time he was hunting. Soon, he would return to battle. Now, it was time to rest and share food among family.

John brought his plate and sat with Jeremiah. "Jeremiah—thank you for helping us stay safe through the storm. The mountain is quiet now, and our enemy lies vanquished and rotting. I don't know; I have a feeling something else is coming our way," John said as he took a slow, small portion of food into his mouth. It was as though he only took it because he knew he had to, not because he felt hunger. Jeremiah noticed his reluctance and knew his words were serious. It had been two days since any of them had eaten more than a few quickly consumed crumbs taken from thin, soiled pockets while crouched in cover.

"Would you have me set out north to spy for more? I am happy to do that, John, and return quickly if I see anyone."

"We have to do that for a time—maybe for a very long time, Jeremiah. We need to see enemies long before they are close to our people."

"Yes, John."

"I wanted to ask you what you thought and how we can best do what is necessary. I don't expect anyone to do all the work while staying out of the village too long, and I am not one to tell people what to do. We'll share the burden."

"I don't mind, John. It's a constant fear. We can't let them be tormented and killed by bad people. It's that simple."

"I know how you feel. I've seen what you did, and I watched your bravery. It's the same as I feel. Without the wisdom of Stars Light, I fear we have lost too much. He would know what to do."

"Yes, I am a better man for having known him," Jeremiah said, placing his plate of food aside and lowering his head. "His knowledge of the spirit, his love of freedom, his love of this village—his example of hope—it was all a man should be, all a man can be. God, I miss him."

"So, let's eat and rest for a time, Jeremiah. I'll take the first watch," John said.

"I'll attend with you, John. One more thing—we brought back all we found and laid it out in the work shed. There are a good number of weapons and much ammunition that might be helpful to our braves."

"Thank you, Jeremiah. We'll look at all of it later. I pray we will never need it—or anything we have that kills. But what many human beings have become will not allow us peace," he said, turning toward Katherine and Sara, who were serving more bread to the party. He thought of these two as evidence of the few hundred men, women, and children of the village who were set for the worst fate—the terror of a violent end for nothing more than the food they worked hours to prepare. John felt the overpowering surge of drive within his spirit, mind, and body to protect them all.

Their only hope was for the warriors to achieve victory over all comers. It was life or death. It was as simple as that and nothing more. He and others would have to kill with no more regard than doing a job, nothing more than that. He wondered whether he would have the strength to continue or when he would exhaust every bit of human strength and become too weak to win, allowing his knowledge of evil to visit the village. He wept at that worry, the knowledge of human limits—his limits that every man faced at some point during the days.

Jack took some scraps from Jeremiah's hand—one of many servings his partner would feed him—and seemed to show a smile. He watched his dog stay next to his side, wagging his tail, moving his head back and forth toward him in happiness. The man knew the dog would go with him rather than be forced to remain behind. Jack followed him when he left to guard the space around the village. Jeremiah and Jack finished their meal, washed it down with some cool water, and rose to walk the miles beside their mountain.

"Time to go, Jack. Do you want to come with me?" Jeremiah said, smiling at Jack, who seemed to listen and understand.

"You're going out to the perimeter, aren't you, Jeremiah?" John asked when he saw the new warrior strap on his weapon again and pick up his small pack, half-filled with tracking supplies.

"Yeah, it's time for me to return to watch, John. Do not worry, brother; please rest. Jack and I won't let anyone through," he said with a smile.

Dobey and his army were coming fast, determined not to slow down or stop until they reached the last landmark reported by Raymond before all communication ceased. The trail of smoke from their engines lay back horizontally against the earth in black, bluish, and white streaks. The Captain sat in the passenger side of the lead truck, his hatred in full throttle.

Ostam's Lieutenant Harris had led his troop into the land once known as Illinois. The army moved across the barren landscape, finding little of value thus far in the adventure. The view he had was bleak in his mind as he sought the promotion he desired above all, but he had only been on the hunt for a few days. He had not come across any people to conquer yet and no other signs of life. He thought that surely soon, he would find something—some resources—something he could bring back to Baltimore and his master, Ostam.

Jeremiah led Jack away in the dusk when the light was such that he was able to move without being clearly detected by any remaining enemy. It would be dark soon, and he and Jack would have complete cover. He followed his instincts—using the imprint firmly fixed inside him of every trail, every slippery place, every downed tree, and every undulation of the landscape. That gave him the advantage. His senses were acutely tuned into his surroundings. He listened, used his sense of smell, and looked all around. Jack stayed by his side as he made his way toward the road.

Dobey was leading his caravan at the same time and was just under one hundred miles north of the village but coming toward them. His hatred for Raymond reached a level within him where imagining killing the man slowly became his entertainment on the trip. He thought of nothing else than dealing with all those who deserted Ostam and were part of his troop. He planned how he was going to punish Raymond—slowly and as painfully as possible—while the noise of the trucks radiated across the countryside they were passing. It was the only sound.

I'll start by taking his feet—one foot at a time with my blade, the pig! Then I'll take his hands the same way. I'll tell him that he can run away. He laughed out loud—poor little pig coward Raymond won't feel like doing a lot of running on the end of raw bones. He laughed louder. His driver didn't ask him what he was laughing about. The caravan barreled down the roadway toward the site of Raymond's last stop.

Jeremiah surveyed the north road and turned to stare into the twilight covering the south road. There were no signs of invaders who had escaped the battle, but he knew they could be out there somewhere. He thought there might be some of them planning their next attack—he also knew that next time, it wouldn't be done the same way. In all likelihood, they would try to sneak into the village at night, killing and taking what they wanted in the confusion. He turned toward Jack, watched him as he walked a few feet away from him toward the north, and stopped, rigid and silent. Jeremiah felt a sudden surge of fear electrify his stomach and chest as he stared at his dog.

"What is it, Jack?" he asked the air toward the dog. He pulled his .44 out and felt the grip of power in his hand. He walked the road northward toward his old house that sat beyond the horizon and wondered if it was still standing or had been destroyed by the invaders. Okay then, he sees something or senses someone. I'd best move to the side of the road where my silhouette will be harder to see.

For man, there will always be other men who would enslave and control—other men who kill easily for some purpose of their own design. Greed drives the worst. His father taught him about the past and what some men did to others. The history, those awful stories, were unfolding in his lifetime and not so different from every other man who saw it in their time too. It never changes. It never stops. The fight, the very real fight for freedom from the yoke of others, was to be forever waged—a perpetual cause of death and destruction. The same war was fought in every generation because man is not good on his own. To Jeremiah, that was a truth that would haunt shallow man for as long as he exists. Of that, there can be no doubt.

This was his time to join the battles. People from the north had tried to kill his new family. He prayed to the God his father taught him about and asked Him to give him the strength and courage to do well in any fight he had to engage in to save the village. Jeremiah knew He had been with him as he squeezed the trigger steadily and took out a number of invaders. He was steeling himself for more to come. Jack had just told him that more were coming.

Chapter 9

"What news is there from Harris?" Ostam demanded from one of his helpers in the court.

"He's gone through Illinois and found little of value, sir," Sands said, holding his hands together as if in prayer. The older man had been one of the soldiers when Ostam consolidated power in Baltimore with his small army immediately after the days of the great lights and fires. "He's found a small group of people by following a thin stream of smoke rising from the central part of the city known as Indianapolis, with some goods and skills. He had to kill a number of them for they were obstinate." He paused to think of exactly the right way to say what he had to say to the grand decider to avoid suffering his displeasure. "Master Ostam, he is set to bring back several who can assist us with our vehicles."

"Get word back to him that he should leave no one alive in Indianapolis when he leaves the place. I don't need him to bring me any of them!" he screamed.

"Yes, sir, I will dispatch a messenger tonight. Your will be done, sir."

"Very well, Sands. Can anyone here tell me about Morford? I'm still waiting to hear from him."

"I'll have to send a courier to find them tonight, Master Ostam," Gack said under the constant angry furrow of his brow. Gack was a second elder who had been with the power from the beginning, as well as Sands. He was a more violent man than Sands, who also had a desire for the young in ways that only evil can pursue. Gack kept several young boys and girls as his slaves.

"Dobey should be near Raymond's location within an hour. He will compensate that thief rightly," the master said as he smiled smugly, his eyes penetrating everyone in the room as he warned them too.

There were consequences for anyone who had the audacity to challenge his authority over them and take from him what he designed.

"We'll turn Harris toward the Carolinas too if we have to, to make sure this problem is resolved," he said to Sands. "Bring the women to me! I am retiring for the night!"

In Texas, Morford sent another patrol to follow the path their dinner ran. The two men he commanded to hunt it should have caught up to it, yet he heard no shots. He sent six more men to find them and the deer— somewhere just over the horizon, he figured. The fires were ready, and the camp was set. One night of food and rest, and then he would continue on his quest.

"We'll know soon if the area beyond that rise is contaminated and what happened to those two sorry feet," he said as he keyed the radio that connected him to the patrol. The group had been assigned to an underling who volunteered for Ostam's army several years ago. The young underling was Frank, who opted for a life with the power rather than fight it and suffer the slavish life of his family—and their deaths.

Frank had a couple of the men in his charge walk far ahead of him while he watched with the three remaining. He watched them closely as they went toward the rise and over the horizon only to see them fall within seconds of each other and not move. Yes, there was contamination over there. We can't go any further, he thought as he used a telescoping device to notice the carcasses of the deer and the two rotting bodies of the men who had gone earlier in the day. There would be no venison tonight. Frank returned to Morford's side quickly.

"We have no choice but to go around west and pass this place," the Captain said. Ostam would not be happy with the time delay. He had seventy men left, plenty to complete their mission and return to Baltimore with food, fuel, gifts, and machines that worked. He was now anxious and nervous. There was no time to rest and eat. He had to get the army on the move now.

"How are we on gas, Frank? Go around and find out from every truck. We have to move and move quickly. Check the cans and make sure we have enough to make it to the large cities and back."

The humans who survived the great fires left in Houston numbered thirty, and they had banded together for survival. There were a few other people scattered across the once-great state who were scavenging as best they could—as Jeremiah did in Carolina. They were isolated, hungry, and desperate, living with only the hope of something to eat and a little water.

Morford led the train of vehicles another twelve hours toward Houston and could make out the outline of many gutted buildings, their exteriors still standing as monoliths bunched together, quiet and dark. He thought he saw a small light somewhere deep within and smiled. We have life in there, he thought. Then, just that quick, it was gone as the caravan rounded a long curve of road. He knew it could simply be the angle of his travel—where now the life hides behind a structure.

As they came closer, the roadway was crowded and filled with rusting vehicles of all kinds. None had much color, and each had been reduced to nothing more than a hollowed-out frame of weak and brittle steel. He knew what he saw in the distance was a good sign.

He halted the convoy and had his men check the hundreds of vehicles for any gas that may still remain in the old tanks—often the last piece to go to dust. Their next move was to head directly for where he saw the light and find out who was in there and what they had. Then he could return home to enjoy the rewards of his find. He would have any woman he wanted after she was cleaned up and he enjoyed the feast he deserved. He had his mind on a nineteen-year-old whose hair was golden, with a full body still, large lips, and most of her teeth intact. He fancied owning her as long as she looked that good to him.

Morford stopped the caravan again once he reached the first set of buildings, where he could guard the vehicles with an open field of view to their rear. The old city was to be explored and taken by foot patrol until he found the source of the light. "No lights. No fires," he commanded his army. "They know we are here, but they do not know where. We must find them first," he said. "Frank, take twenty men out this time and head southwest. I want thirty of you to follow me into the center."

The snake-like processions walked into the city, searching for anything of value along the way. Frank led his group parallel to and to the left of Morford's platoon. He left a guard of close to twenty well-armed men at their vehicle camp. Six hours passed when Morford sensed an odor—an aroma of a cook fire that was close. He stopped his patrol and made them all crouch down in place. Then he led a smaller unit toward the aroma, running and jumping to stay hidden behind structures, with one man kept directly in front of him—just in case there were guards or a sniper.

There was movement. A figure suddenly darted on the other side of fallen mortar and concrete and disappeared behind the corner of a building. He looked back toward his unit and had them spread in a flat line covering two blocks. On his command, they would move toward the next street.

"Ready, let's go," he said. He heard shots as soon as the right flank came across a few people huddled inside the burnt-out front portion of an office. He saw the fire in the center of an old Houston square, where once there was a fountain and brick inlaid walkways. It was a clear area downtown that was once used by businesspeople and shoppers to traverse the newest development of shops, offices, restaurants, and bookstores. He watched as several figures scrambled for cover at the sounds of gunfire. Then he moved his part of the line into and across the square, firing at every target of opportunity they found. Several bodies were strewn about before him as he led the army onward and captured the square.

There was some bounty left by the people who lived there. He saw stacked boxes, blankets, clothing, and a well-designed cooking area, complete with smokers, sinks, and large cutting boards on clean tables. Across the way, he noticed what appeared to be some kind of classroom set up just inside the face of a building. There was more movement.

"Pour your fire into there!" he commanded his soldiers, pointing toward a space between building corners. "Leave no one alive! Move out and get them all!"

A youth of about twelve suddenly appeared with a sword and attacked the soldiers. His body was cut in half quickly with a single burst from the soldier nearest Morford. They finished the sweep and eliminated all the defenders. It was time to take an inventory of their acquisitions and send a messenger back to Baltimore with the news—and receive Ostam's decision on whether they had enough to return.

"Check every building, box, and all the piles for two blocks out and report what you found," Morford said. "Frank—you've earned the right to be our messenger and return to the center with our report. Enjoy your time back there, but only stay one day."

Laid waste were the few men, women, and children left of old Houston. Now reduced to nothing more than garbage left on the streets to rot, eaten by scavenger birds and wild dogs. None had a name anymore. None would make any new mark on the new world. They had no chance. They were not with Ostam, and so they were all just clutter and nothing of more value. There were a few who escaped and moved well away from the killers—and were still moving, quickly and quietly—as far away as they could run and remain unknown to Morford.

"Bring the meat to the cook-fire," Morford commanded. "We will eat after the list is made, men. We have much to celebrate."

Jeremiah ran back to the village to report what he knew before he returned to the range of space that was his to guard. Jack followed him and kept up easily enough. When Jack ran, there were no signs of a damaged leg.

"John! There are others coming toward us from the north! I'll go back and watch for them to sound the alarm. We must be ready," he said as he saw Katherine's face—swallowed in her strength as she came toward him without hesitation to deliver a drink of water to him and Jack. We must win. It is for her, the children, the old men here—we must turn away any invaders who would do them harm.

"We'll form up, Jeremiah. Did you hear them—what did you see? How many are there?"

"I didn't see them or hear them, John, but Jack must have. Jack knows they're close. I know he's right."

"I believe that, Jeremiah. I believe it is from the same people we put away and will have to fight again. But there's a chance they are a different tribe... we don't know who they are yet—whether they are only travelers or those who mean to do us harm," John said.

"You know what's more likely, John. I can see it on your face," Jeremiah said, his voice trailing off to quiet. Both men knew the world as it was now, no longer a nation of mostly good people but something else that murders; the monster of evil, blood its life force. The core of man and all of his historic cruelty was on full display, in full action since the days of the great light.

"I know, Jeremiah. Thank you, brother, for returning to tell us," he said as he looked at the ground.

The ammunition controlled by the village was a finite amount to use for their defense. Even with the bounty taken after the first battle, it was still finite. There were no manufacturers, no stores, no way to replenish except for what others had salvaged and brought to use against them. All the shells were thirty years old, and the crates found in one of Raymond's trucks were of the same age or older.

"We'll need to make ready sooner now, John."

"I'll get on that," John said as he motioned his hand toward the warriors still in the lodge. The twelve knew what he meant and quickly took to their feet, moving to prepare the ammunition and weapons, checking, clearing, and loading new rounds. Word got out to other warriors in the village, and they did the same. Within a few minutes, John had a gathering of ninety men and forty-four women who wished to join him as warriors. He asked the women to stay in the village—but the forty-four couldn't be dissuaded. Jeremiah took to the forest again without Jack this time. Katherine held Jack for him. His canine partner couldn't come with him this time.

The moon, seen through a dark orange sky, was now straight up and over the village. The full moon that night appeared to be orange itself but fixed with a glow behind the cover of Earth's atmosphere. Jeremiah was soon at the road and noticed what he knew had to be light at a far distance. Someone was definitely coming. He fired his .44 into the air.

John had the warriors spread out across the face of their mountain. He hoped these new strangers were not the same as the last. He prayed they were not the same while his spirit was torn and distressed. His heart told him they were the same—killers, takers of freedom, men at their worst in all that had been learned through time about generational hate and greed.

Jeremiah took up a position behind a downed tree near the bottom of the slope of the first mountain, overlooking the road. He waited in his concealed position to watch as the lights slowly grew larger in the distance. He noticed a reflection off some of the steel left by the first army that found and attacked the village. Maybe they'll pass and go south, he thought. Maybe they're friendly, he hoped. He watched the larger convoy barrel toward him and slow at the obviously newer vehicles left there rather than the hulks that had weathered for years. There were more vehicles this time.

Dobey and his army stopped at the accumulation of vehicles he recognized through the weak attempts to conceal them. He knew they were Raymond's, so the traitor must be close, he thought. Jeremiah watched him get out of the lead truck and walk slowly toward them, carefully looking inside each cab before turning to the men near him and saying something he couldn't hear from his distance. Dobey noticed the battle damage and knew what had happened.

"He ran into trouble here," he said quietly to those closest to him. "Looks like we've got a problem here—and we have the solution too," he said, his smarmy smile revealing stained teeth and his intentions. He would hunt and kill whoever did this and still look for Raymond and his men, whether dead or alive—and take whatever these interlopers had. He figured they must have a good haul for Ostam since they were able to stop Raymond.

"Send Stevens back to Ostam with the news and tell him that Raymond and his party have been hijacked and killed—that we're on the path to verify and eliminate all those responsible—of that he can be certain. We're going to hunt them all down and slaughter them like the dogs they are!"

Jeremiah could make out many figures moving around through the glow of the invaders' vehicle headlights that had been left on. Dobey had his army move the convoy toward a nearby defilade on the other side of the road in a clearing where they were protected by the shoulder's gradual and sustained rise. Soon Jeremiah could only hear voices that were more distant; he could no longer see much of the group of strangers. The vehicles were now out of sight and their lights off.

He had seen enough to know that there were many more invaders this time. He felt the same fear he had felt the first time he had to defend his cabin after the days of the great light. It was the same gut-wrenching nerves he experienced when he faced invaders with Stars Light and John last week. He had to return to tell John quickly and silently.

Every stick, rock, and other objects on the ground screamed out as he passed over them, making noise that reverberated in his mind. I'm bringing them with me! he thought. They'll kill all of us—our people—our children in camp, Katherine! It'll be my fault! He made his way to the top of the mountain.

He stopped at the crest of the mountain, turned his body back, and heard no more sounds, saw no movement. Still as one of the trees, he stood, listened, and watched, frozen for any sign he was followed. He remained in one place for twenty minutes until his mind was satisfied. He prayed that he had been too far away for the noise to be heard as he ran up the mountain.

Jeremiah raced down the inside slope of the third mountain and reached the winding stream in the valley that separated the two. The stream made its own way, a beautiful life-giving force with no definite form, moving around obstacles, not through them. He thought of it as a more powerful force than the rocks it converged on, glancing off in its fluid run—covering them when the flow was thicker from the rains that fed it. It was powerful and peaceful, only becoming violent when forced to by the rains. He began the ascent of the second slope, carefully calling out in a whisper to the warriors John had put into place.

The youngest warrior, Paul, was the first from the village to recognize Jeremiah. He stepped out from his cover and said, "Jeremiah, it is me, Paul. You are at our lines, sir." The fourteen-year-old was now an experienced fighter and had survived the first attack. He listened to the elders intently. He learned from them over the last year how to hunt game, and if the time ever came, how to fight human beings and win.

"I must find John, Paul. Please, tell me where I may find him!"

"Yes, sir, he's in the center," the youth said, pointing toward the right side of his position.

"Thank you. Stay down and cover, Paul."

Jeremiah ran across the sloping ground until he came to the area where John should be and called out for him.

"Here, Jeremiah," John said loud enough to be heard.

"There are many this time, many more than the first, and I think they are from the same army! They have stopped at the site and are getting ready to try and find us," Jeremiah said as John handed him a cup of water.

"I see. I feared this. The dead have left too much. There must be a body of people somewhere north of our village, and they may be able to keep coming."

"What should we do, John?" he asked.

"You say their number is great?"

"Yes, I couldn't count, but there has to be over one hundred—and maybe doubled. I do not know for certain, but the invaders may number more than we have warriors."

"Are they coming our way?"

"They're gathering and waiting, John."

"Probably first light when they'll track and hunt us," John said, his voice edged with a tone Jeremiah had not heard before. "They'll have little trouble finding paths to the stream. Then it's only a matter of time before they have the paths to our home."

"We have only a few hours to decide what to do, John."

"Yes. Help me please call the warriors together for we must ask each one of them to again put his life on this mountain."

"None will refuse, John," Jeremiah said as he looked toward his own weapons.

"You're right, Jeremiah, but this time our best course must be to surprise them at their home. We must know for certain their intentions—a tough thing unless they attack and fire upon us."

"I know, John. I've been defending my home for years since the day of lights, and rarely have there been friendly visitors, only people wanting to take for themselves."

"I know, Jeremiah. It is most likely these are the same way," John said, rubbing his forehead hard, kneading against his skull with both hands. "Since we agree, I will tell our people we must go to the base of the far mountain."

Jeremiah stood and began gathering the warriors from the east side of the slope as John gathered those on the west side. The small army soon formed a mass where all could easily hear John's voice. He began by telling the braves that the numbers of strangers were large, larger than the last group, and although there was still some doubt, it was likely they had bad intentions. He asked them to consider their lives—this time, the losses may be great. "And that means many of you will die—women, children, and the men. We see great suffering on the horizon because of this danger to our village. We see the losses now and can't stand the thoughts of such; we may lose some—many—of our beloved here tonight."

Suddenly, a streak of light with a thick white tail that followed it crossed the sky above the mountain, causing some eyes to turn up, soon followed by everyone's gaze. The spectacle, though far away over the forest, gave the army enough light to see each other's faces before it escaped over the horizon.

"We'll go toward the road and close in on them to scare the truth from them. No one shall fire upon them unless they give us reason. There has been enough death in our lives already, and if it's possible, we must put death behind us for it lives with us forever and haunts us," John said. "As the light first comes on them, we'll ask them why they are in this place."

"I must go with you, John," Jeremiah said quietly to him alone.

"Let's move," John said to them as he led the way to the stream and the mountain nearest the road. The small army quickly ascended the mountain and reached the top, looking down toward their destination. Dobey had no idea there were other people nearby and was sleeping after their celebration feast. For John and the villagers, the last part of their journey would be easier.

Chapter 10

Jeremiah thought of Katherine. He longed for a first kiss. He imagined the sweetness of holding her body next to his and her holding him back. It was much better than having to stay in the forest for hours—where time never seemed to end. He wanted the peace he would have with her.

The color blue returned to his mind; he could see a blue sky. He envisioned clean skies and white clouds, heard birds singing, and felt the clean, cool breezes of a world at peace. He thought of his parents and the Holy Bible—how precious the book was to them and how much they had taught him about its contents.

The Bible contained every answer within its pages. So much love and peace is revealed there, alongside the arrogance, hatred, violence, and lust that are not loving or peaceful—lessons about what man is at his core if not guided by the spirit first. Life would be simple and grand if love resided within man and nothing else as powerful drove him.

He chambered a round in the rifle he carried and checked his .44 to ensure its cylinder was operating properly and fully loaded.

The village army was now at the wood line just off the road. Seeing no guards patrolling the stranger's camp, John had the army move in a line toward the mass of trucks and vehicles aligned closely in the defilade. He stopped them at forty yards on the same side of the road and had all the warriors crouch low, becoming small targets.

John and Jeremiah walked closer to the camp and stepped into its perimeter, knowing it might be their last steps. One of Dobey's guards, who was supposed to be awake and watching, stirred just enough to see two figures standing inside the camp. He lowered himself in the cab of the truck he was using, furiously rubbing his eyes to wake up. He reached for his weapon, slowly raised its barrel toward the open window, and then lifted his head enough to try to sight the unwanted visitors again. He had to do something, or Dobey would kill him for sleeping. He pulled the trigger as a warning as soon as the muzzle cleared the air.

John looked directly into Jeremiah's eyes as if he were conveying something to the new warrior in an instant. Both men turned and ran back to their line. The villagers knew to move toward the defilade and unleash a barrage of fire into the camp. Surprise was theirs, and the day would depend on their trust, courage, and continuous fire.

It's hard to kill. It's unthinkable and too hard to take the life of another human being for most people.

Many of Dobey's men began returning fire—wildly at first until they could make out targets. Most of the invaders were unsure where the attack was coming from in that first critical instant. The determined warriors of the village cut down some of Dobey's men in their confusion. Dobey had his army turn and charge toward the road. He had no choice but to kill all the people who stood in his way, whoever they were. Ostam would surely have him killed if he didn't and lost.

The lines of the villagers reeled from the wall of gunfire coming at them. Many fell in the thick dust and smoke rolling toward them, a searing edge of eternity for many. Many screamed in agony as the hot projectiles tore into their flesh. There were legs, stomachs, and faces being hit hard. Paul fell early, instantly, when the top of his head was torn off as if dissected by a sword. The quiet one, Victor, also fell, his voice silenced forever.

Jeremiah happened to see the young warrior as he was fatally struck across the forehead. He watched his body fall back and down as if shoved over by a gentle breeze. John could stand no more death and suffering of his people, and as he took a shot to his upper arm, he waved them all back toward the woodline. He began pushing as many away from the battle as he could reach, demanding retreat—furiously pushing and pulling them to save them. "Find cover behind our trees!" he shouted from his diaphragm as hard as he could muster from deep within him. The battle was not going well; the price of their war was nearly too much for John to bear. The village and he were in a terrible place.

He knew the village would be no more if they failed to stop the attack. The peaceful, loving people of the tribe could be annihilated, as millions had been taken before them when the world exploded and took them, peaceful or not, with it. They had been a most blessed, fortunate few who settled in the mountains. The village had grown larger over the years through births and wanderers like Jeremiah and Katherine, whom they found to be people with a conscience still. Their tribe expanded with people who had knowledge—who knew right from wrong—who lived rightly and were unequivocal about that. Those who chose right were welcomed into the tribe to find a home in the village.

Stars Light and the elders had the vision and the knowledge to understand freedom and lead a new civilization to growth and prosperity.

Each man and woman brought their own talents and skills, and with the freedom to use them for their own purposes, enriched the village's life on earth. Through inventiveness and hard work, the villagers built a life beyond mere survival, beyond just living. The village enjoyed food, clean water, materials for clothing and soft beds, light, education, and even entertainment. There were sports games and contests, feasts and awards.

There were working animals and beautiful buildings that protected the people from the elements. There were teachers, carpenters, doctors, weavers, firefighters, hunters, and farmers. Singers, artists, brewers, and writers provided what they could to ease the pain of being alone in a new world. Each exchanged with others for what was needed. The village had grown to become an oasis of progress and growth. It had become a happy place for its people.

John looked out across the tree line at the hundred or so men and women with him. He knew everything was up to them. Stars Light and the elders had started the tribe, using the Great Spirit as their guide and the Holy Bible as their text. John understood that in ancient times, the Israelites often faced the same horror—the threat to their very survival—by overwhelming numbers of an enemy bent on their destruction. He knew that divine intervention saved them.

So he prayed. He spread his arms wide and gazed toward the heavens. The warriors with him saw this and did the same. There were over a hundred voices calling out, not out of desperation but out of faith and remembrance. Should the Great Spirit answer in a way to deliver them, those guided by good and not evil would live on. Should He not save them, they would surely perish as so many had before them. John knew it was not his earthly, human decision regarding this, and his heart and spirit were ready to accept whatever He allowed.

Each man and woman knew that their inheritance off this earth upon death was a blessed promise to be the sweetest, the greatest reward, and that each would live on in a new form. They understood that without faith, there would be no inheritance. Therefore, it would be according to His will, not their own. In Baltimore at the same moment, Sands fell dead without warning, showing no pain. The senior aide to Ostam fell to the floor the same way a sack of pig meat might be dropped.

Watching these arrogant unders retreat, Dobey knew he had them now and could destroy them—finish them all—and then take their treasures back to his leader. He expected to receive his rewards of promotion and women.

"Attack these animals with trucks in the lead for cover. I want drivers and one man riding and firing as our army follows. Kill them all!" he commanded his lieutenants. He turned to the soldiers nearest him and loudly proclaimed, "Kill them all! Leave not a single under standing!"

He positioned himself behind the swollen ranks, well protected by their bodies, and ordered the army to move toward the forest line on the other side of the road. It will be a short exercise with plenty of blood exploding from these unders' bodies, and I will step on their entrails to clean my boots, he thought.

"Let them spend their lead on our steel! Let's get them, kill them all!" he repeated in a voice as forceful as Satan himself.

The dark, murderous mass moved toward the tree line where the village warriors waited, slowly bringing their hands to their weapons. Each man and woman of the village easily found targets, took aim, and squeezed the triggers of their assortment of rifles and pistols, unleashing a wall of flame accompanied by a deafening sound. In an instant, the moving trucks were halted, and row after row of attackers fell dead. One rapid series of volleys finished the battle in a mass of blood, broken bones, and torn bodies, unable to fight any longer, some taking their last few breaths before life escaped them. The village won and repelled the latest threat. Dobey saw what happened before him and quickly realized he had lost.

There were only two dozen men from Baltimore left. Dobey recognized his mistake and determined he had to run away—west—far from the track Ostam knew he had taken a few days prior. His life in the city of his origin was over, for he would surely be killed for his failure.

"You must return to Ostam," he said to the survivors. "Tell him what happened here and tell him I was killed. You can keep all I own back there. Tell him I'm dead and rotting!"

If the men did that for him, he would have more than enough time to escape Ostam's reach, he figured. If the lie wasn't discovered within a few days, it would give him plenty of time. He knew that once Ostam was informed of the lie, it would mean death for all two dozen. He understood they had to return because they knew nothing different or better to do. None were any more intelligent than an underling. He smirked at the thought of their fate. He would run away without them and travel as far as he could—he took a truck and several containers of fuel, leaving his men to make their way back to Baltimore as best they could. He would drive and not stop except for fuel.

The cowardly captain turned the wheels as fast as the engine would allow and took off toward Texas.

Dobey underestimated his men. They let him go but would not do as he commanded. They knew Ostam would not accept such weakness. They knew he would feed them, their women, and children to the pigs. After Dobey put a mile between them, they began the march to the place once known as Florida. They would surely find food there in some form, even if it meant taking human unders for their survival.

John and the rest of the warriors watched the enemy retreat. They allowed those who would leave peacefully to return to where they belonged. The sight of most of them was pitiful, devoid of life, with no more breaths, no more pleasure or pain. The dead piled before them like refuse, and nothing would be heard from them again. They were struck down because of their intent, and there would be no more chance for any of them to know and think of peace—of what life could be, should be for them. One moment of violence was all it took. One fearsome wave of His hand through the warriors, and they were taken out of the world. The village defenders remained silent after their enemy's collapse. The few survivors fled quickly and were no longer a concern for John. He would let those who ceased trying to harm his people leave in peace, giving no chase, somehow knowing no fear of the invaders who were spared this day.

Jeremiah knew the work that had to be done now: burying all the dead with respect and dignity, moving the hulks of vehicles into the defilade to rust away in the years to come—a reddish testament to man's failed attempt to conquer where his worst desires were stopped again. He bowed his head and offered a prayer of thanksgiving.

Are we to be forever attacked—for who we are? Must we always have to kill those who come? We want to be left alone and live in peace—then why do some desire to deny us that—those with different ideas on the value of each life, on the best way to live? What is it about some men that drives them to risk their lives for power such as that?

John had to inform each family of their tragedy. Each lost heart that surrendered its spirit to God needed to be reconciled through tears and prayers. The burden was heavy, and the words did not come easily as he humbly approached one family after another during the longest day of his life.

Sara stepped toward the young chief and supported him as he made his way to each family to tell them of their fallen members. They had given their lives for freedom. They had made a stand and would not let those who loved death win. Their beloved family members sacrificed their lives for their sake, for the greatest cause—stopping all designs that would kill or enslave them.

He made his way to each of them, and each embraced John, and through their hurt, their grievous loss, smiled at him. Their smiles told him that it was right. The warriors did what they had to do, and many had traded all their tomorrows—every breath, every bit of strength, and life itself—for the great cause of freedom, the love of the tribe, their last sacrifice out of their humanity and decency.

The flag in the village was lowered to half-staff. The village understood honor. They recognized the importance of honor and respect, the need to remember each of the brave souls who perished and were surely now with Christ in heaven.

Morford led his caravan out of Texas to return north. Confident he had done Ostam's bidding, he felt prideful and joyous over his conquest, as though he had led the battle against powerful enemies for the new empire built by him and Ostam. He envisioned himself standing next to the great man, who was all-powerful, all-knowing, and deserved the status of a great leader. Now, Morford saw himself as great and imagined one day taking all power over the city.

Their trucks were loaded with a good bounty, a satisfactory return for their expenditure of fuel and time. No lives were lost in the venture that were worth anything and could easily be replaced by other unders eager to rise in status and favor. Followers were easy to find and plentiful there. The curve he took around that desert-like area was wide—miles away, with plenty of safe cushion for his haul. He imagined his welcome as a hero.

Those who escaped the slaughter were well outside the city, hiding in rubble and ditches in the countryside, too afraid to move. They feared the hunters who came to their downtown camp and slaughtered so many would find them.

Their generation and those before them had a life created by the government of the time. They were some of the descendants and beneficiaries of the once-large recipient population who were provided everything they needed to live through the industriousness of others. The few were now nameless, leaderless, and without knowledge. Death would come to each of them. The last of them would starve after all the others were eaten, as fear and ignorance were powerful forces. They were unable to return to the city where they had relied on the work of others for years —but there was still some food left. Now, much of what remained had been taken.

In Baal, Ostam leaned back in his giant upholstered chair and lit a cigar.

"Sands was a good man. Too bad he's dead," he curtly said to his court. "Do not feed him to the pigs. Bury him near the river instead."

Morford was on his way, and Ostam anxiously awaited the treasures he was bringing. "Good Morford has done my work well. Let him be an example for the rest of you!" he proclaimed. "I will show you how a man is treated who does the good work of our state! He is your teacher now! When he arrives here, make way for him and feed his army well!" he said. "Rachel, check your stable!" He would reward Morford with several of the prettiest women.

The dancers began their performance for the 'great leader,' moving to the rhythms and tunes provided by Ostam's group of musicians. He noticed one dancer in particular as she moved her legs and body with smooth, seductive precision that delighted his eye with her distinctly deep and captivating curves. She was a beauty, and he wanted her to attend to him for the night. Her name was Mary, and she had come to kill Ostam to stop the murder of the innocents.

Mary had named her last baby girl Jane and was denied even the respect to bury her when the city had the infant killed in a horror, murderous nightmare that still haunts her. She didn't have those few moments to hold her during her last minutes on earth. She was only a one-month-old child when Ostam's soldier threw her to pigs to be eaten alive. She didn't hear her last few screams of agony that she must have surely felt. Her precious voice was still small, and the few moments of weak sounds were all he left to the world.

Since that day, she had observed the leader's attitude every moment of each day. She remembered his cold, hateful face in front of her own as he proclaimed the baby's fate as easily as he ordered a drink. He had the baby thrown to her death for simply existing. With little thought, he handed other men and women over to his court for his will to be carried out as law. The executions were finished quickly in the cruelest way imaginable among the many cruel ways one human being can kill another. She was set to kill the monster.

She had thought of the word "cruel" in the past few weeks since Jane was lost. She understood the word cruel. She knew the word evil. Ostam's face was before her when those words came, and one more: hate. She hated him and had to kill him, no matter if it cost her worthless life. Life for Mary was meaningless now—empty, dark, and in her mind, worse than living. She didn't think of her own torture and pain sure to come for her act—nothing of consequence at all. I'll let the pigs feast, as they will! I'm done in this life! My only purpose of being is to kill this evil in front of me! She thought as her eyes found his, and through the dark blue lenses, she knew every inch of him.

Mary dressed in an alluring tight wrap; her skin shone through the side of the thin crepe. Her body was full, and every inch of her breasts, her legs, and her whole body filled the material as if she used the fabric only for color. Ostam was delighted and made his plans for what he was going to do immediately after their show. He had to have her attend to him.

Her face had been made up as art. Exactly the right makeup was used by the dance troupe director—the choreographer who also did the work of costume and makeup for the dancers provided by Rachel. The sheen of Mary's cheeks and the touch of deep red—nearly crimson— dressed her lips, along with the slight touch added to her lashes and the inviting skin tones used for the rest of her face; the results put her in the lead.

She hid the knife inside her calf, one leg covered by a loose stocking to contrast with her bare other leg, creating the illusion of her already being half undressed. She moved and executed the routine perfectly, not missing a single step as her determined spirit guided every part of her. She could see but, more importantly, she could feel the eyes fixed on her. Mary knew the dance was going well enough to enjoy the moment she plunged the knife into the center of his chest to find the black heart that pumped blood throughout the vessel of greed and murder. She would surely have a chance—one chance—to render him pig food as he did to so many.

Gack noticed her too, even though his usual tastes for excitement and sexual power were different. There was something about her that seemed familiar; he had seen her before among the unders, perhaps. The look of that face was now changed, and he couldn't be sure. He stared at her with a long, fixed study, trying to remember but could not. He shifted his eyes to the food in front of him instead and said nothing.

Chapter 11

"We're close," Morford said. "Signal stop," he shouted. The convoy was within three miles of the outskirts of Baltimore, where he could rightly expect a glorious reception as a conquering hero.

"I'll take the lead into town," he told his lieutenants. "Once we're in, get all the trucks to the coliseum—get them as close as you can to the doors," he said, fearing mischief from other parts of Ostam's defense forces. "We'll offload the goods first under guard and post round-the-clock protection."

As he sat in the front of the first truck, he gazed out toward the unders and their shanties. He'd done well. He was proud of his position and accomplishments. Unders were crowded into a ghetto-like arrangement, far enough away from the center so that Ostam could not smell them but close enough to walk to their work, even if they had to walk a few miles to different work sites. Those few unders who happened to be close to the road as the caravan passed avoided eye contact and quickly turned away in fear.

Many of the unders tilled and kept small patches of crops for much of their food. Smoke from their fires filled the area. The air was filled with fumes and odors that choked those betters who did not have to live with it all. Ostam's five-thousand pig farm, coupled with the unders' cooking fires, produced a constant toxic smoke filled with odor. The product of pigs being fed and those selected remains being cooked constantly for the underpopulation forced a pall over the city as a persistent cloud that could not be moved except occasionally by the most severe winds.

Unders were allowed a portion of pig meats and fats from the city-state. Entrails, feet, scrapings from the skulls, and stomachs of the slaughtered animals were given to them. They cooked and ate it between shifts of work. Ostam had the unders work cleaning and clearing. The days of the great light and fire caused megatons of destroyed vehicles, debris of all kinds, human waste, and torn building materials. Ostam wanted it all put back much as it was before and kept unders to do the work.

The leader's vision was a society and city that thrived in a new, better way—with him as the grand leader, the most powerful and richest man in the whole of the new world. Unders were valuable to him only for their work, and if they refused to work, they simply became feed. For those who tried to escape the brand of slavery the city needed, he had his army hunt them down. Ostam would not have every one of those recaptured killed—only a few of their number. That way, as the spared renegades watched members of their family or friends fed to the pigs as punishment, he reinforced the most effective method of control. Terror was a powerful ally to the great leader. The unders all hated him with a passion but were too fearful of his army to break free in force.

That is what he saw as his greatest work. The sculptures and paintings of his likeness reflected his power—and his own notion of superiority as their legitimate leader. He did not have to feed anyone but did so out of what he saw as generosity. Unders and all others must bow down to him to show respect and love for his leadership. He thought he was, after all, the great leader delivered to the people who survived the great fires. It was his destiny to rule, and it was their purpose to obey. His flag was a simple blue globe with one word, Ostam, prominently embroidered across the lower edge.

Jeremiah slowly pressed toward her, and she gently received him in her arms. When his lips touched hers, he felt and heard the music of happiness, joy, and peace. He felt a warmth from outside of himself he'd never known. The touch took him to a place unlike any he had ever been. The free couple embraced, joining each heart in that best place of gentle, respectful affection—that place where neither wanted to leave—or be without even for a little while. It was their first step towards the sweet sacrament of marriage and family.

Jack eased toward them and laid his head on Jeremiah's knee. Katherine gently patted the dog's head as he licked her hand. Jeremiah smiled at his canine partner for becoming part of the peace and apparently wanting to be part of the love he shared with both of them. They slowly rose, took each other's hand, and walked out of the lodge with Jack following them to the edge of the village. There were flowers growing wildly across a swath of earth that held several pine trees in its firm, rich soil. The air tasted sweet to Jeremiah. His hand that held hers was strong yet warm to Katherine.

"Can it be that we are meant to be together?" he asked her.

"I have not thought love would come to me in these days, gentle Jeremiah, but I think it has. You're such a gentle heart. I believe it's a spiritual destiny for those people who find another, and I'm sure you came here to be part of our tribe—and part of me," she said, her warmth showing in her smile while her eyes fixed on his. "I am thankful that you are here."

"I'm a blessed man, Katherine. I pray for a good future here with you."

Mary felt her chance drawing closer, closer. She would plunge the sharp steel into Ostam, one evil son of Satan, she thought. She wanted to enjoy the moment he felt the pain and realized what was happening to him. He seemed to prefer the closer view he had of her, and that gave her a chance better than she had planned. I have to get to the knife and get to him across the table, she thought. She knew her last hour on earth was close.

As she danced within a few feet of him and reached the edge of the table that separated them, a man came to his side. As she planned her jump across the table, Ostam leaned toward the man who appeared close to her target. The music drew her dance away somewhat, but she managed to stay near him without being conspicuous. She noticed his eyes on her, then toward the man, and then back to her moving body again, back and forth, as the natural reaction of a human pig in the process of building an appetite for more than one weakness.

Stevens made it into town—still an hour before Morford would triumphantly ride in, leading his caravan of treasure and conquest. The table Ostam used to watch his dancers was fully loaded with fruits, meats, and breads. The wines and liquors were placed on the long presentation close to each seated guest in ornate carafes of metal and color. The leader turned a full goblet into his mouth, keeping his eyes on Mary. He did not want to wait for her any longer.

"He's found Raymond, Master Ostam," the courier said, avoiding direct eye contact.

"Gack, have that one brought to me," he commanded the senior court member while pointing to her with a fully extended arm and a single unfolded finger. She saw it and knew her chance was fading.

Ostam turned toward Stevens. "Now, tell me where Raymond is, Private."

"Yes, sir, we found where he had been and how far he got. He made it close to the mountains, an area off the south road about three hundred miles away. He's still searching for him as I report. It's a place where some people fought our army."

Ostam listened, as Stevens had to raise his voice to be heard over the driving rhythms cuing the dancers' routine. He heard the messenger say that Dobey was certain there must be much to bring back.

"He told me to tell you that he should be returning in a few days," courier Stevens said.

Mary listened too. Through the music in the background, she heard him say that Dobey knew Raymond had run into some kind of trouble.

"And that's why he thinks there's a good take down there," Ostam said, smiling over the possibilities. "We'll see."

Someone was stopping Ostam in this country, somewhere. There are people willing and apparently able to fight this monster, Mary thought as she made another turn to the beat and sound of her cue for the execution of a move, this one involving a thrust of her hips forward and then to her sides as the number was almost over. The finale included finishing with a fast split across the floor.

Ostam raised his arm and motioned for her to come to him after the music stopped. Stevens stood by until his master was finished with him. Mary approached his side and controlled her body's sudden urge to evacuate the contents of her stomach. Steadfast and determined, she would kill him now.

"Did Dobey have contact with any unders before you left him, Stevens?"

"No, sir, and I didn't see anyone either. He is set to go find them and destroy them. It is surely finished by this time, sir."

"How was he sure he found Raymond?"

"We found Raymond's trucks shot up and half covered near the start of these mountains."

"North Carolina?"

"Yes, master, I believe that's the place."

"Then Raymond is dead," Ostam said, unconcerned about the men he had taken with him.

"I think so, master. There was no sign of him or any of his men."

"Dobey will take care of it. Rest now, Stevens. Captain Morford is close and will be in the city soon. I want you to celebrate with us when he arrives."

I must find them—those who are fighting the monster, she thought as she felt his hand on her leg, forcing her closer to his side. She felt him move his hand along her leg and swallowed hard to push down the sudden presence of acrid stomach juices in her throat. She had to get out of there and away from him. She had to escape Baltimore and find those fighters. I can do much more to stop him, his people, and defeat every evil thing he stands for if I am part of a larger group of people who are not slaves to this bastard, she thought.

With no other idea about what she could do to escape him, his grip, and his desire for her now, she allowed the contents of her stomach to release, a bitter yet sweet relief. The results of her diet as an under—a few bites of pig entrails, a few leaves, and an overripe piece of fruit—violently painted an edge of the table and his left leg. Most of it fell to the floor next to his seat. At that instant, he was repulsed by the odor and quickly stood up, jumping away from her.

"Rachel, come take this bitch and clean her up for me!" he shouted. "Damn it, woman, feed her something that won't come back up all over the place. I want her brought to me before the night is over, and she'd better be clean."

As Mary rubbed her aching stomach with one hand while holding her head with the other, she thought of Rachel and her chance to escape. She planned to make her way south to the place where she heard the people who stopped Raymond lived. Getting away from Rachel would be the first step. She prepared her mind to do whatever it took to escape from her and all of Baal. It would be hard, but not as hard as knowing what happened to her husband and son at the hands of Ostam and their pigs.

Triumphant Morford saw the lights of Baltimore. He leaned toward the driver. "I own this town," he said as he saw the staged reception. The wide street was lined by unders and by Ostam's men to cheer his triumph and welcome him home. He smiled and waved as the trucks passed through on the way to the coliseum. He dispatched a runner to report to Ostam that all the goods would soon be in place for his inspection.

Several female guards led Mary to the baths, following Rachel.

"Strip off all your clothes and shower quickly, woman. I'll put something else together for you to wear. You're a lucky one tonight, under, that Ostam has chosen you! Start by scrubbing every bit of your wretched vomit off your skin," Rachel commanded.

She only had seconds to act. Mary reached down and quickly removed the material covering the hidden knife. She freed it. It was for her to use as the weapon to free herself. She quickly turned it behind her body out of sight as she heard Rachel tell her attendants that Ostam waited for the one who was filthy inside and out of her under skin. "We have to make her clean… at least to look the part. Get the sheer wrap for her, and that's all. We don't have to waste anything else on this woman," she said with disdain. "He doesn't need her dressed anyway."

The water from the shower was opened full and soaked Mary while she peered outside the stall to see where all of the attendants were working. She saw two of them near Rachel. One was preparing an assortment of makeup and aromas while the other flipped the thin garment to make certain it was presentable. She could hear Rachel but couldn't see her yet. She gripped the knife, feeling every muscle and blood vessel in her right hand near exploding as she squeezed the handle. The tepid cloudy water ran down her legs into the large round drain. Come in here, Rachel. Nothing will stop me! I'm waiting for you, she thought. She left the stall and slowly walked into the dressing room, her eyes steely, fixed on a chance for freedom, the shiny steel blade leading the way.

Both attendants saw her with the knife leading the way toward them. They were underlings of the house class and quickly ran away from Mary's threat, leaving her to Rachel. Both women held their screams to protect Mary so she could have a chance to live. Fighting back like she was doing was rare and meant a certain and hideous death if she was caught. The one look the attendants had of her eyes meant they were not going to try to stop her. They knew she was almost bound to die for it tonight. Both women also knew that they too could be in the same place someday and would have to decide if they had the courage to do what their hearts commanded. It would not be tonight for them, for they held on to the sliver of hope for their families.

Rachel heard the commotion of people moving in a rush and returned to the dressing area to see what had happened. Her first thought was the possibility that something had happened to Ostam's object of desire, and that wouldn't do whatsoever. Sometimes these underlings fall out and die, but that can't happen to her until he has her, she thought.

The woman in charge stepped into the space and saw Mary with the knife.

"What are you doing? Put that down and get dressed!"

"I'll not comply," Mary said one word at a time, her voice in a deep, steady cadence.

"Yes, you will! Now stop your insolence this minute, or you will face severe consequences! You know that! Stop this now!" Rachel said, anger in her voice raising the temperature in the room as her face contorted out of fear—of Ostam, not the knife. She backed away from Mary as the underling came toward her.

"I'll not comply," Mary repeated in the same steady tone of serious defiance. Rachel was to hear those last words she would hear on earth. The woman in charge was soon to face the eternal judge, and there would be no debate, no argument, no pleading—only an accounting. "I'll not comply," Mary said again as she plunged the blade deeply into the center of her chest, where the physical heart pumped but where no other heart had a place. Rachel's eyes reflected that she understood in that instant she was no longer in charge.

Mary felt her faith return as surely as each step she was taking into freedom. She asked God to protect her for this—to help her join the fighters who could end Ostam's heartless and cruel rule over so many. She knew He had been with her all along and that despite the hurt He allowed, He had a purpose in everything, and only He knows. Hers was to do, not to understand. Hers was to follow His path, not her own. James and her daughter had to be with Him in heaven, the best place.

She quickly packed and dressed, taking everything she needed for the journey—for cold weather, for warm weather—and stepped out of the capital building as an equal to any who would present themselves, if they dared, if they happened upon her path to freedom.

As night came, she walked toward the coliseum. No one came after her. She made her way to the large front of the place where Morford made the deposit of gifts and saw there were many trucks still there. Most of the men were still moving the last part of the treasure into the building as she opened the door of the cab of an old black truck, the logo still in place on its side. The vehicle was an old Ford and had enough fuel to take her out of the city and beyond.

Mary did not look at the fuel gauge, nor did she worry. She drove the truck out slowly as her determination had no need to hurry; she was moving as more of a force, not only a mortal being under Ostam's control. No more, no more, the drive inside her had the whole person known as Mary taking freedom and throwing slavery back at the ugly face of Ostam. No one saw the driver, only the shadow of a driver at the wheel taking leave as though its movement was normal business. No guard or soldier thought to follow her or stop the vehicle. The few who saw it moving thought nothing of it.

Ostam and his entourage arrived at the coliseum to study the Texas bounty. He was pleased and sent for Rachel to provide part of Morford's reward.

"Tell Rachel that Morford is due. She's to select three of her finest women for the Captain," he told the Private.

Mary turned south and stayed on the road that would take her to the people who were fighting back in those mountains. She would tell them of the young boy they took from her. She left for him and herself. She planned to ask the fighters to help rescue him from Gack. Numbed by the reality of leaving him behind, she wanted to kill—all of them if she could. She knew to put that out of her mind and focus on driving the truck. She had to find those who were able and willing to do such work of absolute horror, whereas alone she could do little. He was only fourteen and was taken as a slave consort for the less-than-a-man who kept him.

The government had kept her away from him for weeks, and she could not be certain he was still alive. In her mind, she could easily see Gack being ripped apart alive by the very pigs they used to exterminate those who chose not to comply. It had come to this, and that's all. The less-than-a-man must be treated to his own government program. She smiled.

Chapter 12

Another Group

They had a brain, of course, but one that seemed only half-developed. With no love of humanity, no belief in a higher power, or simply no earthly heart for other people, the half-men made their way into Florida as they managed to calculate their escape from the wrath of Ostam.

There had been few survivors in Florida from the days of the great light, and the conclave of those who did survive found the swamps safer. They survived by eating every kind of animal or the carcasses of animals left where they fell, burnt inside from the light. Few animals remained after the light, except for a number of reptiles and the occasional human wanderers that had also become a staple for the new kind of Floridians. The olive and orange-skinned race had come to enjoy the fare—human flesh was especially craved and hunted for its sweet, tender properties that were similar to the long-ago enjoyed pork.

The near-naked population spoke few words—more of a few sounds a human animal can make. The population verbalized very little. They lived much like a clutch or pack of animals. They had devolved into creatures that were non-historic but prehistoric in temperament, man in his most primitive state again, stripped of all those facades of superiority over other animals. Man's greed and base desires had brought these back to the truth in its base and wanton form, before God was known and right was recognized. Man without faith had been catapulted to this place of empty, dark, slightly higher predators.

They were but one of the results of mankind's full circle on earth, following generations of brutal, murderous violence by large numbers—nations—and smaller numbers—producing thousands of pockets of criminals in many towns and cities across the world. Driven by greed, desire, jealousy, and hate—every Satan-inspired human weakness, most humans acted on such impulses for their own satisfaction. The Floridians living in the swamp were the natural result of such progress in all of this, after governments often put vain, violent people above others for generations, leaving some who learned nothing and were unable to live differently, as they became mirrors of those who lived near the beginning of man. After the day of the great fires, many had reached the end of the circle and were beginning again.

Many that were left lived with literally half brains and, figuratively, half hearts. Brains that worked for instinct alone kept them alive. Many whose hearts worked only as pumps of blood and oxygen, and nothing deeper, were left to be led by someone—someone with the mind of Ostam and others. For many people in Baltimore and Florida, nothing was immoral, nothing too vile, and using or killing others meant nothing to them, as their hearts were only pumps.

Now the twenty-four escapees from the attack on the village in the mountains were using their own intuition to find what they could take in a place none had ventured before. The pack of others waited for such travelers with an appetite. The natives first sensed and then saw the feast headed in their direction. The outliers waited in the grasses to see what the entire herd looked like—they had to know how to begin the hunt.

The soldiers of Ostam, running for their lives, found little to scavenge as they entered the land of stripped and barren palm trees. The few palm tree trunks still upright appeared as skeletal remnants of twenty-foot tall creatures rather than the unique, beautiful trees that thrived in the sunshine. Seven sultry days had passed.

None felt or saw the eyes watching them. They had no fuel and were on foot, crossing the flat earth in search of food. They were making only ten or twelve miles each day because they were weak from hunger and growing weaker from a lack of food and water. Every house they entered looking for something had been stripped years ago and was empty. They moved toward a large city that was once known as Miami as they walked along the edges of the swamp that seemed to cover every mile. Dobey's renegades figured there had to be food in Miami.

"Are there to be more to come?" Sara said. She had yet to speak much. After her loss that day on the road, she had turned inward, into her own small world. There was nothing outside she wanted to know anymore except for Katherine and the kindness of the mountain people. The village, the tribe, had proven to her that there were good people. She felt that every good person was prey, though.

"I can't answer that, Sara. I pray there won't be," John said as he looked at her and then toward Jeremiah and Katherine. She surprised him with her sudden words. Since her arrival in the tribe, she had been a quiet, humble presence with Katherine guiding her—much like a shadow.

"Why do they come to kill us?" she asked all of them.

"There are some reasons, I suppose," Jeremiah said. "Some come for our food and water and would rather take it all for themselves than ask— things we gladly share with those who come to us hungry and thirsty."

"I'm happy to hear your voice, Sara," John said. "Please know that you are home now and no harm will come to you here. I hope you feel it's your home. My promise to you is that we'll protect you from those who would take, and God willing, we'll prevail. The power is ours as we have His divine blessing, you know."

"I do feel it as home, John. I'm sorry we've lost many and do not want to lose anyone more. I'm afraid."

"There is every reason to have hope now, Sara, beautiful Sara. Do not worry your mind over matters of this wicked world, for here we love and live for each other and the Great Spirit. We will live on, build a world right here in these mountains, and gladly join with others who are of the same mind. I say surely, there are others who love peace more than war, as we must."

"You call yourselves the Americans. Tell me, please, why use the word?" she asked John.

He looked into her face and studied the concern expressed through her eyes. "Our nation—our village, Sara—is American. We are a people who strive to be what our nation could have been and not what it had become," John reiterated the lesson from Stars Light.

"Aren't the ones trying to kill all of us Americans too?"

"I understand why you ask that—they live in the land once known as the United States—America—but no. In our minds, they gave over to themselves years ago and forgot their nation. They simply are; they simply exist for what they can take."

Jeremiah led Jack outside the lodge as night approached. Fall was bringing cooler air to the mountains. He looked toward the sky and could see a difference from the way it appeared ten years ago and even last year as he watched the vapors of his and Jack's breaths escape into the air.

The earth was healing itself. It would be in her time. Slowly but distinctly, the earth was coming back from man's worst. Someday there would be more new growth trees, cleaner waters, better air, and soil. Man could have another chance, he thought. If we stop wanting to kill each other, we have a chance.

He walked back into the lodge with Jack following him. The dog sensed the change too. Jack was excited and happy, as if he knew what the change meant. Jeremiah opened the doors for both of them with a rush.

"The sky is cleaner! Come see!" he said. The joy was clear in his voice. "We're seeing our world come back!"

In Baal, Ostam was still in the coliseum when the private returned. The younger man was out of breath and trying to speak to him while taking deep breaths to recover when he found the leader near the boxes. He ran as fast as he could to report to him.

"Master!" he said, breathing hard. "Miss Rachel is dead!" He struggled to say between breaths. "I found her in the baths! She's been killed!"

Ostam was furious. "Captain Morford!" he called out. "Get your troops to seal the city! Find out who did this and bring him to me now!"

Every member of the army Ostam had still in the city was quickly put on alert. The soldiers were dispatched to the perimeter of the city. Over a thousand soldiers took up positions to prevent any movement in or out of the center and from the under ghetto and anywhere outside the thirty-block area.

"Find every under who was near those baths and bring them into the hall!" Ostam commanded.

Captain Morford took the men who had been with him in Texas to the wing of the capitol where Rachel worked. He had every under who worked in the building brought to the main hallway and made them stand in line and wait.

The first one felt the sudden sting as the rope trap snapped around his ankle, putting a tight loop around his leading leg and causing him to fall face first into the marsh. His face and torso were instantly wet and coated with a kind of mud. The men with him ran to see what happened, and as the twenty-three stood close to him, forty men of the Florida pack rose near the trap and surrounded them all. The long sharp rods they pointed toward every Dobey soldier were close enough to stop them from using their weapons. They were too close, and there were too many—not the odds they favored in battle. Every rifle quickly dropped into the marsh, where it disappeared under the thick greenish muck surrounding their feet.

Using a series of grunts and sounds, the strange-looking men tied them together neck to neck with a rope and led them out of the swamp. The line of prey was marched for hours before coming toward a large cluster of scraggly trees, bushes, and huts of sorts. It was the village of the prehistoric, the flat land shelters, and cooking fires they used—the center of the ancients.

The nervous soldiers of Dobey were herded toward a pen. They were guided by the grunts of their captors and shoved by rod point into the pen constructed of logs held together with vines and rope remnants. There was no roof to the place, as livestock needed little shelter that deep in Florida.

As the captured entered the enclosure, they began to notice evidence of former inhabitants. A few patches of old cloth with faded colors, several old shoes now more a part of the dirt than shoes, and a number of hollowed-out, rotting stumps that appeared as though they were used for food troughs. Inside and around the stumps were a few remaining berries, tiny specks that could have been some kind of grains, and pieces of rodents, snakes, and other small particles that couldn't be identified by the soldiers—all used by the pack's previous prisoners.

One of them spoke after the large, heavy makeshift gate was closed, leaving them inside while their captors set about to prepare a fire. "How long will they keep us here?" Most were afraid to ask why they had been rounded up and imprisoned.

"We're not leaving," another said.

"We're food," one of the more intelligent ones said.

In Baal, Morford gathered the unders who worked in the palace. "Tell me what happened to Rachel! You people know and better tell me," Morford announced to the standing crowd of unders, their backs against the tall wall that lined the capitol's ornate foyer.

Most of the people brought to the place did not know anything about the murder inside Ostam's seat of power. Most had not been anywhere near where Mary killed her controller as the first step of her escape to freedom. There had not even been the first rumor, let alone talk of it, from the two women who were close to the incident. The young women attendants were petrified with fear. Even knowing what happened could mean a horrible death, as the purge would start in earnest by the court and the explosive Ostam. The willing murderer Morford was more than pleased with such assignments.

"I can start peeling the skin off one of you and do that to all of you one at a time until someone speaks!"

That was enough to hear. One of the attendants raised her face toward him. "I know, sir," she said, forcing the trembling in her voice to form the words. "It was the under Mary who was being made ready for the great leader, sir. She was the only one near Miss Rachel. We had gone to get her dress for him, and when we returned, she was lying on the floor, and that Mary was gone."

"I see… and you didn't stop her," Morford said, staring hard directly into her eyes. "There were others there too, and none of you did anything?"

"Sir, there were only the two of us, and we weren't in the room with them, please," she said, bowing in a show of submissiveness.

"And I'm to believe you?"

"It is the truth, sir, and that's all I can say. We were not there to stop…"

"Silence!" he screamed, interrupting the woman. "The under who was with you and you… Come with me!" he said, brusquely waving his arm toward her and back.

They both knew they would surely die. Their time in life was over. They knew the others might live on for a while. In tears, they both did what they were told and followed Morford into another room. They both knew the best they could hope for was a quick death.

"Find that woman known as Mary!" Ostam commanded the troops near him.

Ostam was waiting for a resolution, and he was not a patient man. Morford had little time to produce. He returned to his quarters with the female unders and put them at a table where the questioning was to continue, led by him. The killer has to be somewhere in the city, he thought, as he pressed the unders for where she went when she was not working for Rachel.

He held them in his parlor for hour after hour, alternating between leaning over them and shouting questions to having them sit silently, waiting. He was not getting anywhere as every nearby location was ransacked by his troops looking for Mary. The hours began to stretch long, and Ostam was still waiting. He felt exhaustion begin to overtake him. He had had enough.

"Go. Get out of my sight," he said, disdain and hatred clearly evident in his tired voice. The unders could serve no further purpose. "I'm sick of looking at you."

Morford went outside. He breathed several deep gulps of rancid air, sweet to him, and looked out toward the skyline of the city. If she's here, we'll find her. She has to eat. She has to do something other than hide in a hole somewhere. We'll find the woman! She has to pay with everything when we do find her.

"I want a guard at every corner, every area—and forty men in the under village."

"Yes, sir," one of the nearby Lieutenants said.

"And every man had better stay on his feet, moving, looking for this under woman!"

"Yes, sir!"

"Do not harm her when you find the filthy scum. Ostam will decide what to do with her. Do you understand?" He knew that Ostam would have a special torture for her.

"Yes, sir!"

Yes, take your countenance now, woman! Feel like you've done yourself proud. It won't be long now and you will be ours, you'll be our feast of revenge.

and watch your blood seep slowly from your body until every drop has been put on the ground and what's left of you is fed to our herd. Yes, they're hungry, woman. They're always hungry, and you will feed them, one bite at a time, and one swallow at a time, and you'll be gone. We'll let your blood stain a street and leave it there as a warning to every under who thinks of doing such a thing to a member of this court. We'll find you. Your time is near; he thought, as his mouth turned upward in a knowing smile. You're ours now!

Mary was two hundred and fifty miles south of the city when she ran out of fuel. She had to make it the rest of the way on foot and didn't know how far that was. She didn't know the people she was looking for nor how they would receive her—a stranger, and now a killer. She thought of Rachel and what she had done. Was her taking life the same as what Ostam used for his own purpose? Her heart torn by doubt and guilt, she set out toward the deeper south on foot.

She was alone. The sun rose and gave her a view of the wreckage and a never-ending stream of man's pitiful end—all the way from Baltimore, there was nothing but evidence of the result, perhaps the final result of what man had done to himself. There had to be a way—still, she thought. There had to be life in peace and love somewhere, of freedom, of respect for each other, of holding onto the old-fashioned notion that every person possessed their own right to life and dignity. She kept walking, pushed despair aside, and forced her spirit to build hope one small sliver at a time within her mind.

Chapter 13

"Not me!" he screamed at the three nearly naked men who came into the pen to pick one of their prisoners to eat. Two of them reached out and held both of his arms in a grip he could not loosen, while the third man put a rope around his neck to pull him along. The olive-orange men walked him toward the open gate while several others guarded the opening with spears. The other Dobey men recoiled away from him, every face frozen in horror over what was about to happen.

Every man knew his time was coming as they watched him being dragged out, his feet useless, his screams futile, and through the gaps in the log gate, they saw him receive a deep slice across his neck. It was the same treatment chickens receive before being cleaned and put into the pot. The knots they tied around his ankles quickly hoisted his body from a barren, thick tree limb to let him bleed out. Barely alive, the rest of them watched him breathe until his chest stopped moving. A large fire crackled and smoked across the way from the pen.

The captured men watched his dismemberment. Their captors placed pieces of his body on a rack over the fire. It was a sight they had to turn away from to save what little remained in their stomachs. Like others before them, the men cowered against the back wall of the pen and fixed their gaze on the landscape behind them through cracks between the logs. Not a word was spoken inside the pen. Silent tears flowed down each face.

At the American camp, a memorial began.

"Let us honor them," John started the memorial for the warriors lost. Jeremiah and Jack stood at the gravesites with the village. Jeremiah stood next to Katherine, and Jack sat beside him. Jack seemed to understand the solemn nature of the event and remained still. The village ensemble played some old tunes. Each piece was a hymn from the time of their parents and the parents long before them.

"We pray over them, for them. Their sacrifice gives us life. As Little Wolf and Stars Light before them, their courage reminds us all of what American courage is. Our freedom—their freedom—shall always be threatened, for greedy man's nature is nothing if not enslavement. Remember this, family and friends! Remember each beautiful heart buried here and thank them and the Great Spirit for their brief time on earth. Wish them the best reward as promised. They must be in His garden now, watching over their family and friends still on earth. We shall never forget what each of our brothers and sisters did here for us all. Raise the flag back up in the spirit of that, in the spirit of carrying on, of holding to the virtues of freedom and peace. Thank you all."

The mountain had not been as full of life since before the days of the great light. Birds were singing—there seemed to be thousands of them. Insects were chirping loudly again, and on the ground, thick, rich green growth was visible, full and beautiful. Sunshine covered the village under the bluest skies the people had seen in years, and the gentle breezes brought comfort as each villager felt its pleasure through the air's clean touch. Even after the ensemble had put their instruments down, there remained music in the air for the minds, hearts, and spirits of the tribe. The people slowly, reverently left the place and returned to the joy and work of living.

"Katherine, dear lady... will you marry me?" Jeremiah asked as he lowered his eyes.

She firmly took his hand, pressed her gentle smile and face against his. She nodded her acceptance so that he could feel her answer. The couple would have a village ceremony and become a new family of the tribe. John planned to officiate the joining of the warrior and his bride. The marriage would add a new family to the community—and the couple would be united in the best way, loved by the Great Spirit, and cherished by the village.

Morford learned of a truck that left in the early night amid the confusion caused by Ostam while he was surveying his treasure inside the coliseum. He began the party and was playing, happy over what was found and brought from Texas with a single excursion. He thought that if such a haul was still in Texas, then California must offer an even better one. In his mind, he envisioned a larger cache of weapons, jewelry, paintings, food, fuel, and all kinds of luxuries for his taking. While Morford and his troops enjoyed Ostam's reaction and pondered their imminent rewards, Mary slipped out from under their control without revealing her direction and route. The Captain was certain the killer had already left the city with the help of some of their underlings.

"Take your guard, Lieutenant, and follow the path she took out of town. Find her. She can't have gone too far," Morford said while he cleared the pistol he held and returned it to the holster. Ostam assigned the Captain to trail her, knowing he would receive another good reward for returning Mary to Ostam.

Three small trucks left with the Captain in the lead. There were a dozen men tracking her as fast as they could drive the vehicles south. "She had to go this way," he said to his driver. "It's the only road clear enough to make time."

The Captain knew this was one of those missions where success would put him in a good light with Gack—and with Ostam. He thought that he might very well be awarded a rank equal to Gack for it. Where Lieutenants had failed, surely a Captain would succeed! If he could find this Mary—this lowly under, he would bring her back to them and revel in success. "Faster!" he called out. "Let's get her!"

Suddenly, there was a crash. The truck in which the Lieutenant was riding was hit hard. It shook the cab and crushed part of its front bumper and grill. "What was that?" he called out excitedly as they accelerated through the under ghetto.

"Nothing, Captain... We're still moving. I think it's okay," the driver said.

A young teenage under lay crumpled on the street. He was barely moving when the second truck ran over his body. He had been on the dark street looking for his little dog and had just found him before being run down. Under men rushed out to remove his body from the old asphalt, where both he and the little dog that had been in his arms now lay broken in painless death.

Tears were nothing unusual for the village of the unders. Theirs was a usual heaving, deep in the throes of the enslaved, ceaseless torment of being nothing more than a man or woman. Their life was nothing more than a swallow of consuming fear that tore at every impulse inside them. Being a nothing was every man's, woman's, and child's present—their past, and as far as they knew, their only future. It was living in the state of Ostam. Their lives were constant tears. Their minds were constant, shunted things of little particular use or value to their masters. The state had taken all from them as part of the grand design of Ostam's society and rule. One more dead under was as important to the state as one more dead bird—or soldier.

Mary had left the empty truck and walked through to the next day and into the night before she stopped for a couple of hours of sleep. Her jaw felt tighter, and she felt it strangely fixed. Her courage honed and grew stronger as the hours passed. When she awoke, she took some grass and ate it, using the dew as her water and the green sheaths as her food.

The Lieutenant who was driving Morford in the truck that struck the boy knew his mission. Nothing else mattered to him but to find her.

"I think we hit something—an under, Captain. I didn't see it."

"Don't stop. They'll deal with it on their own back there," the officer said dryly, staring at the road ahead.

"She could have gone in any direction once she cleared the city, sir," the driver said.

"I think she would head south, driver. There's nowhere she can go east or north—and west would have kept her too close to us because of the loop. Drive faster!"

The small convoy reached a steady speed of fifty-five miles per hour through each curve and across the hills and valleys.

The boy who was killed had a mother who was still living. He also had a father who worked in the city's sanitation department. The shouts and wails of anguish brought them both out of the hut they shared with their only son. The couple followed the sounds and walked over one hundred yards through the tight maze of huts and houses that lay between their home and the road. Their son, young David, was not with them. The worried couple surged with others toward the gathering crowd.

"It's David," one of the citizens said, still distant enough that the couple couldn't clearly hear the name called out, but the mother thought she heard the faint sound of her son's name. Through the noise at the road and around her, she felt as though her heart was falling out of her chest. It can't be my David. It can't be our boy. The dreaded stream of words ran together in her hearing and invaded her mind, unshakable. The crowd had grown at the road.

Her legs became weak. She could barely stand and was having trouble walking further toward the road. Her arms lost all feeling. She was numb as she forced her feet, one at a time, to take her eyes to the center of the crowd and their migration out of the ghetto. She forced herself to breathe. She saw him and knew it was her David lying on the road.

His father was crying and couldn't stop. He saw it was David—this crumpled, still figure being covered by someone's quilt was his son. The unders were all around the spot that was his last place on earth. At first, the men and women there hoped for a sign of life, some chance for the boy to live. They had hoped for a sign, but it wasn't there.

The lowest class of people suffered another loss in a constant stream of losses at the hands of Ostam's court and his loyal government constituency. The unders were expected to accept the conditions and work for a little food and water, a little warmth and cover from the biting rain and gray snow. There was no choice for those made to be a lower class of human beings that made up two-thirds of the city's population.

There was nowhere for them to go to live better—so they had been told for many years now. If some tried to escape the hell that was the city, that was Ostam's nation, they became prey. Much had changed for them since the days of the great fires. The worst changes had nothing to do with starting over, but with the government that was formed in the city. Earth and man's calamity opened the cast doors of opportunity for Ostam and his few who promised them the lie that would bring safety and care in return for their service.

The mother and father wept, torn up inside, their life taken as surely as if they had taken a shot in their heads or a knife through their hearts.

The one thing they had in life that was a source of joy, comfort, love, and even pride had been ripped away from them forever. The boy was still. He suffered for a minute until the second truck crushed the little bit of life he had left—a kind of final relief in quick order—the new natural progression of things in Ostam's nation.

To curse Ostam and the state would cause more harm to the couple. To reject their controllers and slap against arrogant heartlessness would bring punishment. The reward system Ostam put in place decades ago guaranteed a report to the authorities, who saw all dissent as dangerous to their status and control. Any mother and father who failed to quietly accept all that happened to them as a result of the government could expect a miserable life in the underground system of watery sewage—if life was allowed at all. Everyone was to comply—for life, the rules were constantly broadcast, written, and spoken aloud as decreed by law.

The mother and father held each other as the weak couple managed to return to their hut, a tight space where the four walls kept the world away from their hurt. They both had work the next day, had to report on time, and they would. David would be buried the next day in the leveled acres set aside for disposing of bodies.

Over a thousand others were interned in the place where no markers or headstones were allowed or used—only small artifacts marked the graves of unders. Tiny remembrances of life that were barely visible covered the barren landscape. David would be buried there soon, and above the hole his body filled, the couple would place the only item they possessed for such a horror. They had a small hand-sized crucifix from the past for their beloved, symbolic of a long-ago ridiculed religion that had become a shrunken resemblance of the faith. They marked their son's permanent location on earth with a simple cross.

He saw a dark blur at a distance. One person—who appeared to be alone—was walking toward him in silence. There was no light to guide Mary's way, no one to follow; she came toward him as a steady shadow. He thought it was strange that so soon after the killers appeared near their mountain village, another stranger was making way where so many died. He ran toward her.

"I won't harm you!" he shouted. "I'm here to help you! What do you need, traveler?"

"I only want to pass, sir," she said.

"Please give us time," the furthest watcher said. He sent a runner to cross the mountaintop and relay word to the next and then to the next until John soon learned another human being was coming to the village.

"Very well, I'll find out what she needs and if we can aid her," John said, asking Jeremiah to join him. "Take word back, please, that we will meet her near the road."

Chapter 14

The Captain found the abandoned truck a couple of hours past the old invisible line that once marked a border between the states of Virginia and North Carolina. His analysis of her movement was confirmed, and that made him proud. He chose the correct road. Gack gave him the job he thought he deserved because he was the smartest officer of all, picked by Ostam for even higher office that would be his before any of his peers. Only Harris was in his way.

Mary slowly approached closer to the man. He wore a dark leather shirt and dark trousers. His long black hair was held in place by a simple headband. The rifle he had slung on his shoulder reminded her of Ostam's army. His look was different, though.

He was different. He talked to her as a respectful human being—found only in the under colony to some extent, some sincerity. She saw and felt it. She knew she had found them through her controlling determination and all-consuming passion for justice someday, some way. Reaching her goal was never in doubt to her. She found the people who had fought the organizer of Baltimore and won. It was obvious to her since it was he standing there, and there was no sign of Dobey and his men.

"Our Chief, John, is coming to meet you, Miss," he said, the politeness in his tone obvious too. "Have no fear, for we do not harm travelers who mean us no harm. Where do you walk from?"

"I escaped Baltimore, sir—once a great city, now a prison. It is Ostam's city now, and he's a tyrant among tyrants." She turned her head down. The thought of the mountain of walls guarding justice began to sink her some. "I wish to find the people who I heard turned him away, sir."

John, Jeremiah, and Jack made their way through the last few feet of the tree line near the road. The watch had their visitor seated, sipping from his canteen of fresh water, and taking a few bites of dried fruit and potato.

"They were from Maryland? I've heard of Maryland," the man said as he saw John stepping toward them. John heard her words. He wanted to know why so many came to kill his village, the tribe who believed in peace—who welcomed strangers with an extended hand, not a knife.

"Yes, I am too. It is a horror there, sir. It's hell. I lost my husband and baby and have a child in bondage to one of the court members, as they are called—those who do his bidding, whatever he decides and decrees so cruelly."

"You're welcome here. We know nothing of this place of which you speak," John said, studying her face.

"I heard there were those who fought them. I must join them. I must be one of them. Is this the place, sir?" she said, speaking to John.

"It was here," he said. He thought that she may have smelled the blood near the road the same as he did still. "I can see that you have come a long way. I'll take you to our village, where you will have food and rest. You're not a prisoner with us. Be certain of this, dear lady… you can leave if you desire or stay if you wish."

Jeremiah listened to her story. She survived the great fires as an infant when her father placed her and her mother in an underground shelter he built deep in a state known as Pennsylvania. The rolling hills nearby provided just enough airflow so they didn't suffocate as the wave passed over the landscape. He heard her describe what happened to them when they made their way south searching for food. He heard her describe what happened to her baby and husband and believed her. It made him cry in despair within himself.

Katherine and Sara dressed Mary's wounds from the injuries she endured during the journey. They served her good cheese, bread, and the cleanest water she remembered ever tasting. They heard her recall the real nightmare and cried aloud. How close they had come to the same fate shook them; both felt the electrical pulse travel unobstructed from their feet to their heads.

"They may be coming for me. That's what Ostam and his court would do—for their reason or for no reason—that's what they do to people," she said, pausing. "I don't want you to suffer because of me."

"You can be home here, Mary," John said.

"Thank you, sir."

"It's John, please. I am John to everyone in the village." He smiled. His strength of character and courage were evident to her in his angled jawline and bright, clean eyes that were unflinching, clear, and knowing. John knew at that moment that the fate of the village had changed; there would be war to end the conflict strangers had begun in the mountains of the village.

"I'm Jeremiah and this is Jack," he said, smiling to ease the pain he felt for her while he stroked the dog's back. He asked her about the son left behind. "He must be brought here, Mary."

"I know I should not have left him," she said, turning her face down in shame. "My purpose was to find the fighters and join them to destroy everything Ostam," she said, a look of shame coming over her face for being selfish to think others would help her.

"You would have been killed, and your purpose—any purpose of your life—would have been lost forever, Mary," John spoke up. "Please, don't worry. I hear you, and we'll take up your cause for it is just. I believe you are honest. If I were in your place, I would want the same for what happened and for all those poor people enslaved by a cruel man— only a man after all, nothing more."

"I can't really expect you to risk your lives in a war with those who are so far away. I'm sorry for thinking that way."

Jeremiah turned toward John. "The first thing we must do, John, is get that boy out of there," Jeremiah said. "I'll go and find him and bring him to his mother. One has a better chance than many." He felt the power to do that. From deep within his heart, he knew this was his next purpose, his next mission. He could not fail.

Word came that vehicles were coming toward them again. The Captain was leading the convoy slowly to catch sight of the straggler he was sent to find. Capturing an Unders woman should be easy. Unders weren't very intelligent—certainly not like him—and finding her would be easy at this point, he thought.

As he approached the large number of Baltimore's trucks, he figured she had made it this far, so he had his convoy stop to probe around the area. There would be signs to find that would lead them to her, he thought, and it wouldn't be long now. Then he could return home successful.

The watch for the village saw them coming and sent word. He watched a few of the strangers step around their own vehicles and then into the divide of earth that took them out of his sight. He saw a few others, including the lieutenant, walk toward the tree line where he waited. These were the men sent to capture the woman, he thought. She was afraid they would come for her.

It would take a long while before anyone else from the village would be there to help. He had to either stay in place or retreat up the mountain. The watcher peeled back and slowly began to make his way uphill. Distance, I need more distance, he worried.

Jeremiah prepared for his journey north. There was plenty to do— and getting there would be another very hard job. There were hundreds of miles in front of him and then back again. More than a journey, more than a simple focused quest, this was a chapter in his and Jack's life, a major chapter in which the cost may be weeks of his life if not life itself. Presently, there's no more worthwhile cause I have to work for, he thought, and there's no better use of my time.

He took his .44 along with a rifle and a full backpack that covered the length between his neck and hips. The leather coat he had was sewn with a thick liner for the cold. The hat was a floppy thing that he could use to protect his ears from the cold when the time came. He was kissing Katherine goodbye when the runner came to tell the village of the new threat on the road.

Jeremiah had no plan. He didn't know yet how he was even going to make it to Baltimore. He knew he had to go and do it alone. He planned to leave Jack with Katherine and the village as a whole, which adopted him like every pet was adopted and cared for by the people and children who lived there.

The runner from the foothills told John of the strangers. Jeremiah was just beginning to step toward the pathway down the mountain when he saw him. He stopped to listen. His journey to find Mary's son would have to wait.

A group of armed warriors descended the mountain along with Jeremiah, who carried much more on his person than the others. Captain Morford found a large swath of footprints and bloodstains. He didn't know what to make of it but thought Mary must be near. He felt eyes. Maybe they were hers.

"Let's go this way," he said, leading his soldiers toward the first mountain. "If you see her, do not shoot. We must bring her back alive."

They followed the widest trail up the mountain where the ground was well-worn by feet and movement. The leader of the hunting party knew she would have used the easiest trail to run away. The sides of the trail were bordered with broken and trampled growth of all kinds, from seedlings to vines, brush, and dirt-covered limbs and leaves.

He led his troop to the top of the first mountain without interference —and found no sign of the escapee. He thought she had taken flight in these mountains to hide. She probably watched the vehicles coming for her and ran away this way from him. He knew they had to be close to her, and a little while longer, a few more steps into the forest, and he would have her, Mary's pursuer thought.

"I hear them. Quiet now," John whispered as he listened to several men climbing down the slope of the first mountain, breaking twigs as they stepped, making such noise that the echo clearly signaled they were coming. John and the braves were at the top of the second mountain and listened to their movements. The men from the city could not be stealthy enough to escape detection. The environment was not what they were accustomed to, as asphalt and concrete were the usual surfaces of their rule and their battles.

John had them wait, concealed, blending into the background and becoming invisible among the growth and trees. The line of twenty warriors was set up as a defensive line, waiting for the strangers as they walked right toward their concealed positions. Should the strangers climb up the second mountain, they would have spent even more energy and strength—they would be weaker for the fight and lose like those before them.

Learning from Mary about the nature of the men who were the Chiefs of the city, John had little doubt what the travelers would be inclined to do on first contact. He knew no chance could be taken; they had to be ready to fight again. Fighting seemed to be continuous as many men were living history's script and would never stop to change the paradigm. The young Chief learned wisdom from Stars Light and knew the world to be a sad place for most still—that even the days of the great light had not been enough. No event would be enough. Man was determined and bent on destruction. Being that way in their hearts, his own.

Destruction was bound to follow. Freedom and peace were illusions found on the sparse few islands of enlightenment—true enlightenment, not the false kind that enslaved. He passed the word to be ready after he made contact with their leader.

The warriors heard them climbing up the slope, weapons and gear clinking against their equipment and uniform buttons, now a louder giveaway to their location. Jeremiah eased the large pack off his back and set it aside for a while. He joined John to descend the grade toward the group of men. Both knew they were likely not friendlies. To assume the worst about their purpose and intention, however, was a grave sin, an injustice. The strangers were nearing the American tribe and village, which meant they would have to answer to the Chief.

As the Captain leaned back against a tree trunk to rest halfway up the path, John and Jeremiah stepped out toward him from above and startled him. He didn't expect the sudden appearance of armed men so close, particularly one who had taken direct aim with a large pistol at his heart. With no signal or sign indicating anyone was that close to his patrol, he jumped up, his sidearm hanging limply by his side.

"Who are you?" he demanded, feigning strength. "Where did you come from?" His neck twitched involuntarily, causing his eyes to dart around the two figures that had yet to say a word. The Captain's men slowly, groggily, stood up from the spot of earth they had used for a temporary rest. They hesitated, and several took a step further away from their commander.

Morford shook his head from side to side to regain his full alertness. He raised his arm slowly, gripping the pistol tightly, watching for any movement from the two strange men who had stepped into his space on the side of that mountain. Jeremiah was quick, bringing the barrel of his . 44 into direct line with Morford's face the second time he raised it. The Captain lowered his arm. These people aren't compliant, he thought. Inexperienced with such confrontations, a sudden flow of urine darkened his trousers. The men he brought with him stepped further down the slope. The ambitious commander dropped his pistol on the ground, and it slid partway down the grade. Morford knew these were the people who had stopped the army the first time.

"What purpose do you come to this place?" John asked the trembling stranger.

"I am searching for a murderer—a woman."

"There is no murderer here. Turn away and go now, and you will not be harmed."

"Signs show she may have come this way. Have you seen a woman with blonde hair, about thirty-five years old?"

"I have told you the truth. There is no murderer here."

"Do you own this mountain?" the Captain asked, feeling safer as his instinct for control reactively overpowered his fear. He thought better of it just after the words left his mouth, but it was too late. The large pistol barrel was suddenly and quickly pointed directly at his forehead.

"No. We do not own a mountain—no one can—nor shall you take ownership. This is our home, and you're not welcome. Listen to me… Should you bid this earth, the price shall be grievously high, and you still cannot own it. Go now. Return to your home."

"There's a killer near here, and beware if you don't allow me to find her."

"Go now and live," Jeremiah said. "Last chance to hear me!"

John touched Jeremiah's extended arm while staring into the Captain's eyes, as if to say hold now, give them a chance to leave in peace. Morford turned toward the descent and led his few men slowly away from the two menacing figures. He pushed low branches out of his way as he walked back in the general direction of the road—in a kind of half-climb—to get away. He thought he would be shot at from behind, and with each step away from them, he determined they might be the cowards after all.

John and Jeremiah stood their ground above and watched the sight of their retreat. "We can't trust they'll leave as they said they would. Few men are men of their word—especially these men who are in the mountain now from the place Mary spoke of," John said.

"Do you want me to follow?"

"We'll both follow them, Jeremiah. Your journey to this place— Baltimore—waits away from these mountains, and it must be started soon. Please go with me as far as the road and watch the strangers leave our home—and then you may continue your long journey. If they do not leave us, we will all have to defend our home. I pray you will be safe and return to our village soon."

"I'll return with Mary's son, John. It won't take long."

The Captain led his few men toward the road and soon allowed his arrogance to take prominence over his mind. He was certain they were alone since the men who surprised them were no more than underlings who hadn't been caught and taught their place. "They have the woman. I know it!" he said as he stopped them all from stepping further. "We'll double back well to the left until we are on higher ground above the cockroaches." He laughed. "We'll jump them this time and take them out. We must kill everyone we find except that one. We'll find Mary, that killer, and bring her to Ostam for his special court." He laughed again. "Quickly now! Let's go!"

Morford was one of those men who couldn't learn—or wouldn't. Driven by ambition, he led the few up the mountain again, confident in his leadership, certain of his future. He was delighted that he would soon see the blood of the men who startled him spilling out on the mountain slope.

Jeremiah spotted their movement through the forest and whispered to John. "They're going to our right and back up toward us, John."

"I was almost certain they would," John said. "Our choice is made for us, Jeremiah." He looked down and clenched his teeth. There had to be more killing, a thing for which he had no appetite. The way of the warrior was a hard way, a desperate task not for the faint-hearted. Much like a dark sea coming in for high tide, the village defenders covered them all, and the enemies were removed from the world one by one.

No one would hear or see any more of the officer or his men, nor would they think of them. The small party from Baltimore became a very small part of the mountain where the bodies would remain forever. Mary was safe and beginning to learn the village ways, the American ways—the ways of life on the mountain of freedom.

Afterward, Jeremiah made it to the road and took one of their trucks to head north as far as it would take him. He hoped he would get as far as Virginia on the fuel he had—maybe further if he covered every mile slowly. The day was ending, and dusk began to cover the horizon in front of his eyes. The air was becoming colder by the hour and would be freezing soon.

He thought of Katherine. He thought of her warmth and her accepting embrace of a poor survivor whose father taught him some things about living—about finding food, loving others, being wary enough, and remaining trusting enough to respect others. Mile after mile, he drove with no plan other than finding the boy and taking him away from this Gack fellow. Time now, patience, alertness, be smart, Jeremiah, be strong, he thought. Think first, think last.

The blackness of night covered every direction and hid the landscape all around him. It was hard to see the road. Years of neglect erased the white lines dividing the lanes and marking the shoulder. All he could see was the old concrete and asphalt directly in front of the truck's dim lights. Much of it was crumbling; large spans of road were little more than rocks and dust.

His speed slowed as he pressed northward. An old map had the marks of the two-dimensional roadways, the general picture of paths—including the abandoned interstate system of his ancestors—the path he needed to reach that city. An occasional faded sign alongside the roadway confirmed he was traveling toward Baltimore.

Mile after mile, he rode on as far as the fuel would allow him. He had to get as close as he could to the prison where the boy was being held by these people. Many people in Baltimore thought they could own another human being. He remembered John's admonitions to avoid going alone, but risking others in this service was not in Jeremiah's character. He thought of finding the boy and taking a vehicle to escape the city, getting them both well away from this Ostam tyrant. Jeremiah knew that once he was outside the city with the boy, he would make it back to the village. Once he was free of the concrete and steel prison, he would be able to evade and survive with Mary's son in tow, keeping him safe as well. He knew how to survive; honed skills over the years had brought him to this job, and it was just another job. He was well prepared to finish the work.

The road seemed to disappear completely in front of him. It's time to rest now, he thought, as he turned off the desolate stretch to park the vehicle for a few hours. He left the cab to find a nearby place and cover his body with one of Katherine's quilts. He laid the .44 next to his chest. It was sleep, a little sleep accompanied by a gentle and distant serenade of life resurging. Life now was greater since the day of death. The skies had finally begun to clear. The morning would come, and the path to the prison-city would be clearer.

Chapter 15

Harris gathered his finds—treasures and people with skills that would be of service to Ostam. His caravan was over halfway back, and every man with Harris was relieved to have been assigned this search. Their forage mission west went well; there was no battle where the risk would have cost them their lives. They had taken a good bounty. Soon they would be with their women and off the road.

Once in the city, Harris had his men unload the human bounty. Bound to each other, the line of captured men and women was twenty strong, tethered by rope, and appeared healthy. Not like that one time in the past year when several had died on the road back. Ostam looked at the collection of his new unders and began his planning.

"I have work for you here," he said to them as a group. "In exchange for your work, you will be fed and put into a place where you will be warm."

The skills and abilities of his people had dwindled over the years as teachers in every field died out, and few were trained to replace them. Ostam stepped toward the first man in the line. He was elderly but had a crust of hardness about him. The old man still had thick arms and a strong-looking back. "What do you do?" the leader asked.

"I'm a mechanic," the man said. When he spoke, many teeth were obviously missing—evidently, half of them had rotted away over time. His white beard was stubby but clearly white. His head was half-bald, and the hair he did have was stubby too.

"What do you work on, old man?"

"My name is Lee!" he said defiantly. "Cars, trucks, diesel, gas, compressors, boilers, pumps—you name it, and I can fix it, but not for you! To hell with you people!" he said, his grin and curl clearly telling his captors he was a man who would not go quietly anywhere they wanted him.

"You're an insolent old man, aren't you? I'll see you do our work or it's simple… You'll die quickly," Ostam said. He stepped toward the second man, with Harris standing close to protect him against any possible attack. "And you? What do you do?"

"I teach mathematics. I also write and cook, sir," a middle-aged man known as James said. James was a helper to the people left in Indianapolis, having worked closely with Sara, who stood bound next to him.

Together they had found food and the means to continue the supply by cultivating and growing crops. They had kept heaters going against the winter cold over the past years for everyone in the city by fueling a single turbine and generator, then controlling just enough power to feed one electric heater in each of twenty shelters. The disaster of the days of destructive lights did not stop them from regaining a foothold on life and sharing that with the people who were alive after the fires.

"Very good," Ostam said as he turned his face toward the woman who was tied to him. "What about you?" he asked one of the two women in the group, Julie.

"I'm an electrical engineer. My specialty is generating power, transmitting it, and controlling it for use."

"You'll have plenty to do here," he said and smiled. "We have only one station, and our coal supply has nearly run out. Within six months, I need you to help find another fuel and convert it. Can you do that?"

"I believe I can, sir," she said, the word 'sir' escaping her lips reflexively, causing her to gag, but she forced the word through. After enduring the under squalor and its odor, she had a sense of this city and the rules of its leader. She knew she was a long way from Indianapolis.

Ostam returned to his large office—an expansive, rich space that was the size of twelve hobbles in floor space and filled with paintings, special rugs, and statues of his liking. Gack attended him along with several court members who were just below the old perverted man in importance.

"We'll use them, Gack. If there are any who cannot be of service, send them to the unders."

"Yes, sir, of course."

"I want our next investment to be a doctor. Old Killian is getting to the point where we may lose her soon. We have to have one to do the job. Population control is becoming harder every year, you know."

"Yes, sir," Gack said. "Maybe she could teach others how to do it."

"She could. Her refusal to do that has become troublesome. She knows she is the only doctor."

"I'll meet with her again, sir."

"Convince her. Tell her that I personally promise no harm will come to her after she's prepared others to take care of pregnancies we don't want."

Jeremiah was outside the undefined gates, the unseen barrier that separated the city from the free nation. He missed Katherine, Jack, John, and the village, and felt alone. One job at a time, he thought. To find that young boy so he can enjoy freedom is worth anything I am—anything I do.

On foot, he came upon the distant sight of a ghetto. The odor swept over and through him. Mary was right about everything he had heard her say. The evidence was before him. He knew from her that he was not to trust anyone because in such human desperation, any one of them would turn him into the keepers for Ostam. Mary would still be without her son. He had to carefully pass the area as one of them, an under, remain nondescript, and make his way to the great hall as she described to Jeremiah to find Gack. Where he found Gack, he knew he would be close to finding the boy.

He observed them from a distance and quickly ripped his clothes to mimic an under. That night he slowly crept into the ghetto undetected and took up the place of an under as his disguise. With dirty and worn clothes along with an old floppy hat, he appeared to be one of them. When he was sure, he stood and meekly walked through the odd village, cowering near its edges, finding as many shadows as he could to further disguise his movement as a stranger.

He left his pack hidden in the brush well away from the collection of makeshift houses and took his .44. Hiding it inside his trousers suspended by a rope, he carried extra ammunition wrapped in cloth to silence it. He smeared mud on his face and hands. The rifle was camouflaged to appear as a large walking stick. That, combined with his dark clothes, made him just another unseen figure wandering through, thinking of nothing but the next meal. He had a few miles to go.

At the northernmost edge of the ghetto, he saw the first of Ostam's sentries. Most sentries were once unders themselves before being accepted as keepers. He stopped and watched them, not moving any part of his body, remaining inconspicuous as he melted into the landscape and background of squalor. He reached down and felt the hard steel of his justice maker. He would kill them all if he could and set these people free, but patience meant survival as their numbers were such that he stood no chance in an all-out fight. What would cause people to accept being slaves like this? Why do they not fight and throw off the masters themselves? Why do they stay? He thought, feeling both sympathy and a kind of absolute anger rise up inside him.

He turned his face toward the village behind him and watched a woman lead a youngster across the main dividing line between rows of huts—their only sort of road. She was bent, and her little one was being pulled along behind her as a dog might be if leashed. She appeared like the others he saw: colorless, a sullen figure, and hunched over from hard work. She was nearly indistinguishable from the huts and scraggly bushes. She was no longer an individual but merely part of the filthy, fetid background, without hope, without ambition, without an idea that life could be different. Her one offspring allowed would be the same as her, he reasoned. His stomach knotted up. He cried over the thought of such waste in this world as it is.

I've heard about this, he thought. People can become like these and give up their future, never thinking they could live better. They just live for what is given and accept it until they die. Many may not know of liberty or even the word of God. It's pitiful. It's evil what people can do to other people and their generations.

He watched the guards and moved toward them, taking cover behind one abandoned hulk of steel after another—old cars and trucks that were left where they stopped, many in the same place they were abandoned during the days of the great fires, those brilliant yet disastrous lights. Jeremiah moved on one of the guards when he turned his back and took him out with a quick deep cut to his throat. The guard wasn't able to shout out and give him away. He watched the man bleed out as he covered his mouth tightly to stop all sounds. The second man who had been with him returned from relieving his bladder toward the under-village. He was quickly choked and taken down to the ground, where Jeremiah held him until he too moved no more. He took uniform parts from both of them to fit his body enough to pass as one of them. He collected their weapons and checked both of them for ammunition and operation of the bolts and receivers. He threw the rifles over his shoulder by their slings and headed toward the section of town where the keepers lived. It was a good start.

"Find Stevens and bring him to me," Ostam said to Gack, who would in turn delegate the job to another one of the captains. "There's been no word from Morford either! It's as if every man I send down there is sucked up by something and dies. I want to know what the hell is going on in those damned so-called Carolinas!"

Within weeks, there was only one man of Baal left in the pen in Florida. The last man watched every other man who took flight with him to escape the judgment of Ostam be taken and killed. One at a time, they were removed from their pen to be cut, cooked, and eaten by these human forms. He was their last human food source, and his time would be over soon. He put a few insects in his mouth and crunched them to swallow. He followed that with a few pieces of a kind of wild grain and grasses that the olive orange men gave him. It helped kill the taste. He turned his face toward the warmth of the sun, squeezed his eyes tight to see as much of the sky as he could. He knew that soon it would be his last time. He felt a sliver of relief surge through his body.

Later, he heard the steps of a large group of men coming closer toward the pen. They were coming for him. He pushed out his memory of the screams he had heard before from several others as they were being prepared. He turned his face toward the sky once more and fixed his brow upward, sipping the last bit of sweat that rolled down his skin. Soon he would not hear the awful sounds. He would not hear mouths and teeth gnashing for flesh against bone and tearing it away this time.

Chapter 16

Ostam felt more fear than ever after the burning of the former nation. He was now convinced that another city was as powerful—or worse, more powerful than his. There was at least one army defeating his armies down south, and he didn't know how large they were. Could they come here? He worried, he wondered, he was unable to think through what was happening inside his brain. His body convulsed.

Fear was constant for the leader. It drove him every day, though he never acknowledged it. Inside his greed, fear was the fuel that burned hot, unsusceptible, crouched deep, and coiled, transformed into his own definition of brilliance in his mind.

"Gack, Morford was our best—our most trusted captain."

"Yes, sir, he served our city well and never failed."

"Tell me then, where is he? Why have we heard no more from him?"

"He's bound to be gathering riches from the south, sir. He'll surely return with plenty of fuel, food, and many goods."

"Unless he is no more, Gack," Ostam said after a long nervous pause.

"We have no report of that, sir. I trust he is taking time to gather all he can for us before coming back."

"We have no report at all, Gack."

"May I ask what you are saying, sir?"

Ostam turned away from him. Even though he did not care, the sight of him nevertheless sickened him—but he needed Gack's organizing skills and political influence. His habits, though, were an aversion to the leader. He began to quietly hate Gack more.

"First it was Raymond, then Dobey, and Stevens said they found his trucks—no sign of him and his army. Now Morford is in the same place, and we have no more word from him. What am I to conclude but that there is another army capable of attacking us?"

"It's possible, sir. So… we should avoid that area, perhaps. We have the rest."

"It's they—whoever they are—they may be strong enough to attack us here, fool! We must grow our army quickly. We've lost three hundred men to those people! Take a count of how many we can add, Gack, and be quick about it! We have no time!" Ostam said—the disgust toward Gack clearly evident in his agitated voice, a sound that mixed fear, anger, and impatience. He was shifting his voice between loud and nearly quiet.

He didn't know the fate of the captain sent to find Mary and suspected his failure to find her ended with his death. The forces of independence were rising. He was unable to conceive of such a thing and did not know that either. The forces of freedom and right were gathering strength in spirit through knowledge. One soldier of those forces was in his city, wearing the uniform of Baal and closing in on his headquarters.

Jeremiah had no trouble finding the main hall. The seat of power stood as a monolithic testament to the old when politicians surrounded themselves with the best of everything. The old system allowed them to take and take some more to feed their base of power and their own greedy, unquenchable appetites—their insatiable desire for power and the trappings of power. That power was a power over people, disguised as doing the right thing for the people even as they lived in squalor. Now Ostam was one who knew he was destined to inherit that power, and no one could change that!

Jeremiah saw the guards. Over time, the men who guarded Ostam's castle had come to take their duty with a large measure of a cavalier attitude. Nothing happened most days—the murder of Rachel by a stranger being the last event that caused even a ripple in their routine. Day after day, shift after shift, there were no thieves trying to get in to steal or anyone trying to attack the court or Ostam. No one dared until now.

The American warrior walked straight up to the two guards standing near one of the side doors. He chose that entry since there were many more guards at the top of the front entrance—stationed at the top of wide, steep concrete steps as broad as the building's face itself that led to a garish multi-door entry. The side door was simpler.

"Who are you?" one of the guards asked the approaching soldier he didn't recognize.

"I am Zack," he lied.

"I don't know you. What company are you from, and what are you doing here? You're not on duty."

"I have come to relieve you both," Jeremiah said, giving them a chance to live.

"There's no order. We cannot give this post to you," one of them said as both leveled their rifles toward Jeremiah. He was quick and raised his hands in outrage. The extra rifles shifted to aim at his chest.

"What are you doing?" Jeremiah shouted, and as soon as the guards heard the words, he plunged a long knife into the center mass of the guard closest to him, causing the rifle to fall with a loud clatter against the concrete beneath the feet of a slumping man. He whirled and caught the second guard from behind, locking his throat with a strong forearm as he brought him down, taking him to sudden, permanent sleep. In less than two seconds, he cleared his path to the boy who was somewhere inside the block-sized building. He pulled the bodies away and hid them both inside the first door he found that opened. Okay then, now what, Jeremiah? he thought as he straightened his ill-fitting uniform as best as he could. He stowed his collection of four rifles behind a desk positioned in the narrow hallway of the entrance for use later if needed. He was prepared to defend the boy to the death as they quickly made their exit.

He prayed for help. Doing that was not something he had to work to remember. It was as natural as breathing and part of him. Whether his Lord would send unseen guardian angels to protect him and the boy was uncertain—especially since he had killed other human beings and might kill more. Still, he prayed. The boy deserved a life, he reasoned; he did not deserve any kind of abuse from anyone, and no one, including Gack, had any right to claim ownership of other human beings. He knew well that no one has a right to take over another's life either and that this government, purposed solely to protect Ostam, had no right to exist. It must someday be destroyed for the sake of the people—either when it eats itself or when liberty-minded people finally rise up to take it.

Pulling at his uniform shirt and slinging one rifle over his shoulder, he walked down the passageway to survey the building and learn its layout. Taking one step at a time, he moved ever closer to the center. His mind and eyes were sharply focused on all that lay in front of him. He moved as a man not of his own mind but instead as if drawn inexorably toward a mission, a feat, a rescue.

He felt hot air with each breath. It was from his own heart and not because of the coolness in the air. He felt the sweat seeping out of his pores. He heard voices nearby and walked straight toward the sounds. Where is Gack? Where does he keep the children? Give him over to me! Tell me, man! I will kill if I have to and take on the heaviest burden a living man can possibly bear in his mind and soul. I've already got many on it and am not afraid to take more!

He saw a couple lounging ahead. A woman and a man—both appeared to be dressed elegantly in the finest silks, satins, and brushed materials of which he had no knowledge—were sitting together. Another man approached them, seemingly serving the two. The stranger watching them was suddenly standing and hovering while donning the uniform of a soldier for Ostam.

As the couple talked and smiled, Jeremiah was suddenly in their space, standing close enough to their chairs to feel the armrest of one brush against his legs. The woman looked up and saw the menacing figure, so insulting, so outrageous. It was a violation of Ostam's rules for the status she enjoyed. The man's face contorted into a quick scowl. This soldier would surely be punished severely for such arrogance.

"How dare you, soldier!" the man shouted, anger erupting from his sense of power. He was a third-tier bureaucrat, well-regarded by his master, Gack.

"Where do I find Gack?" Jeremiah asked the man in his deep, steady voice, using his warrior eyes to hold him in place. The third-tier keeper stopped talking and stared back at the soldier. His trembling hand replaced a glass on the small table positioned between the large chairs.

"Tell me, man. Where are the children he keeps?" Jeremiah pressed threateningly. The server began to back away.

"What are you doing?" the woman asked Jeremiah, causing the server to take steps back. Jeremiah stopped him with one hand.

"Stay," he said to the server.

"This is an outrage! What do you want with Keeper Gack?" the woman asked.

"I will see him and the children."

"Is he expecting you, sir? This is most extraordinary, and I don't think I'll tell you anything."

Before the man could continue to say that a soldier like him would be punished for violating protocol in the hall, Jeremiah seized him by the arm, wrenched him up, and pressed him against the hard surface of the interior wall.

"This will get you the death penalty! Release me, you treasonous soldier!" he said, his voice shaking.

"No," Jeremiah answered as he unslung the rifle and chambered a round with one arm.

"Tell me where Gack can be found, or you'll die! That, sir, is your choice… and you will make the choice now, for I have no more time for you." The solemn tone and the directness of his words, like an object falling and crashing to the floor, caused the man to lose control of his bladder. The strength of Jeremiah's grip and the forceful sound of his voice silenced the man. The weight of the strange soldier's words resonated hard, leaving no doubt that he wasn't playing.

"He's usually in the red room," the man said, his voice quivering. "It's down the hall, to the right, and up one flight of stairs. It's the last door on the left. Please do not harm me."

"All of you, come with me!" Jeremiah growled.

He made the three lead him to the red room. Large double doors opened to Gack's wing, where years of accumulated opulence from confiscated luxury decorated the massive room. Neither the senior keeper nor anyone else was inside the main area. Several doors opened to other rooms. Jeremiah made the three sit close together on a plump brown sofa positioned against the back wall. Seven life-sized statues bordered its angles and walls.

The nude figures were reminiscent of Renaissance sculptures, whole and new as if the years had taken no toll on an old artist's work. Jeremiah saw volumes of old books lined up in precise order—not a confused collection of short and tall covers, but arranged in geometric patterns—it was obvious to Jeremiah that the books were not read but served merely as part of the decor. He stepped across the thick Persian rug, passing many gold fixtures, lamps, and the grotesquely sized table in the room's center to open the first door. He sensed movement behind him and quickly turned.

"Stay or die," Jeremiah said to the man who had been serving. He had been commanded by the third-tier bureaucrat to report the intruder in whispers, and Jeremiah had heard it. The soldier forcing them to Gack's lair was acting well out of procedure and had to be stopped from committing such a dangerous act. The bureaucrat did not know what the crazed soldier intended to do—but invading Gack's palace was an outrage. No one was allowed here unless personally invited by Gack himself. The soldier had already crossed the line that warranted delivering his dead body to the pig farm.

Jeremiah returned to the sofa and quickly tore some of the cloth from the woman's dress and stripped the men of their shirts. He used the material to tie their hands behind them and then bound them all together. He tied their ankles in the same fashion and pulled the knots tight enough that no hand could release them. He used smaller strips of fabric to cover their mouths in a final act that would allow him to search the rooms. He leaned toward the trio. "Try to leave and you die," he said in the same voice as the promise he made earlier. "Do not test me again." The third-tier keeper nervously shook his head from side to side and whispered, "I won't."

Jeremiah heard sounds coming from the door directly across the space from the sofa. It was the voices of children stirring; some anxious words could not be heard clearly but were clearly not the kinds of sounds and words he heard from happy children and young people of the village. He quickly opened the door and saw them. Inside another massive room, there were beds and a variety of hanging silks and drapes creating many small Baal sanctums of God-forsaken perversion where the old second tiers could indulge their every desire.

There were young girls and teens dressed beyond their years and young boys dressed ridiculously as even younger children than they were. Jeremiah would take all ten of them to the mountains rather than only the one he came to save. He saw his mission through tears that obscured his view of the grotesque sight of what Gack had done to these children. His choice was quick and easy. He had to get every one of them out of this hellish place.

"Listen, all of you… I'm not a soldier of Ostam! I'm here to take you to a place of joy. Come with me and I'll take you to freedom," he announced with a trembling voice. "Please, you must trust me, God in Heaven, please trust me, and come!"

He heard a commotion outside the room and turned. Gack had returned with an attendant; both appeared to be unarmed. They wore floor-length purple and gold robes of a sort worn by royalty in the past. As he opened the door wider, he caught Gack's eyes staring hard at him. This lowly soldier interloper was invading his space. He reached for a lamp to use as a weapon.

Jeremiah heard him tell his second to run and report the crime. As the attendant reached the threshold of the entry, he was brought down by one shot from Jeremiah's .44. Suddenly trembling with fear, Gack backed away quickly.

Jeremiah turned toward the children. "Forgive me," he said to them as he closed the door so they couldn't see what he was going to do to Gack.

"What are you doing? How dare you murder my assistant! You'll die for this! What company are you from, soldier?"

"Not yours."

The second shot rang out, causing Gack to jerk back and fall to the floor like dead weight. His forehead had been pierced by a well-aimed shot, and the man was no more. The sound, though, would surely bring guards toward the lair. Jeremiah turned to get the children out of there quickly.

As he began to lead the ten young people out of the wretched place, he asked if any of them were Mary's son. One weak voice answered that he was. "Is my mother alive?" the boy asked, his face wet, as his emotions were a mix that had grown over time to explode with fury. He missed her as any man might miss his own heart when his mother is snatched away forever.

"Yes. I'll take you to her," he said. "Now I must have all of you follow me quickly and not stop. You must stay with me! I will take you where you will have a home!" Mary's son felt a new and, until this point in his life, unknown surge of strength, although he didn't know exactly what it was that was moving through his heart and into his arms and legs. It felt good to him.

Jeremiah took them to the stairway and hurriedly led, pulled, and nearly pushed each one of them down the first flight. "You must be quick. You must stay close together," he said, nervously waving his arms to encourage the large group of adolescents and early teenagers. There were bound to be guards running toward Gack's wing of the building even now. He was certain the wrong people had heard and may very well have felt the deep compression the report from his .44 instantly put into the air when he fired it twice.

The night was still young. It was mealtime, and most of Ostam's court and guard were eating the food served to them by under slaves. He had the cover of the night to use once he got them outside the building. He had to get them outside, though, and well away from this center of cruelty. Down the hallway, he rushed and pulled the youth with him, not a word, not a sound other than rushing feet as they barged through the hallway and toward the same side door he used to enter the place.

"Come now! Stay with me!" he said forcefully but quietly. "We must make our way to the next building—stay close to me and the walls. Do all of you understand? You have got to become part of the buildings!"

Jeremiah was the first to step out into the cold air. There were no new guards yet, and he had a chance. He quickly surveyed the space close to them and then in ever larger perimeters outward. He saw they had an opening. No danger was in their path. It was time to run and hide as best as they could and make their own way to freedom. Ahead, he knew the lot where the vehicles were parked in alignment. The collection included some of the cars and trucks that Ostam and his keepers used—and now would be the way he would put some distance between the children and the keepers. He knew they would have to steal at least two of them, and he needed a second driver. He wiped the sweat from his brow.

He brought the group to a corner where small shrubs could provide some degree of concealment.

"Does anyone here know how to drive?" he asked. He listened for an answer and heard silence. None had been taught or had ever been behind the wheel of a vehicle—it was another act forbidden in Baal by Ostam for under offspring. It's even worse than I could know here. These people have slipped the edge of sanity and taken everyone they could trap with them. This is the result of man having no bounds to his depravity. All these keepers ought to be eliminated from the face of the earth! Even if another takes his place, the work must be done again... and again, for all time I suppose. That's what is required of man who believes and what is expected of the imperfect. He pointed toward the boy who appeared to be the oldest. "You'll have to drive with me."

"Yes, sir," the boy said. "I think I can."

"You'll have to, son. You can do it! You must do it!"

He was in front of the group when he saw him. The blocks they covered further away from the center were vacant, but he saw a lone guard at the entry into the lot. He had the children wait behind a brick and stone wall while he solved the problem. "Don't look," he cautioned them as he crouched with them. He stood, rounded the corner, and walked straight toward the guard on post. Jeremiah approached the guard with long, quick strides and a smile.

He had no choice. There was no time to waste. A general alarm could send dozens of soldiers into the air looking for the killer of Gack—and more importantly, there was a man who had the gall to invade the house where all power was firmly in place. Jeremiah knew the person—and the people—who put themselves over others would not yield to such an affront lest others do the same. He closed in on the unsuspecting guard and took him out with one long knife strike to his middle chest and stripped him of his weapon. It was merely a minor delay. Ostam's soldier died before he could utter a word or take a second breath in the face of the children's rescuer.

The oldest boy stared at the steering wheel and the floor pedals. Jeremiah wasted little time teaching him. "Press that pedal to go. Use this wheel to steer. That one is the brake and stops the car when you push it with your foot. When we start moving, stay close behind me. Okay?"

He started the two cars—large sedans once made in the country—and had the children squeeze inside them, evenly divided between the two steel carriages. He turned out of the lot to drive south past the under-village and out into the countryside as far and as fast as he could to get these children away from Baltimore. He needed time and separation—a chance to evade those who might follow him to kill him—and probably every child with him. They had witnessed an escape, and the knowledge that such non-compliance threatened their security, their comfort, their control, their absolute power.

The small convoy broke out of the city unobstructed—a clean swipe through the darkness to the road that had brought the American warrior inside Baal. The boy driving the car behind him was doing well and keeping up. He glanced back to see him within one car's distance of the back of the car he was driving—a gap the boy managed to maintain with a sure hand. He picked the right one. The boy was more prepared than he thought.

Inside the lodge, John and the other elders had been alternating between prayers and hopeful conversations. John felt happiness swell up inside him without prompt or reason. There was goodness filling his spirit, raising that best kind of smile, that best kind of human joy. Jeremiah must be on the way home, he thought.

Jack had taken to lying near the front door of the lodge for hours at a stretch, waiting for his master. Katherine made certain he had water and food, but he barely touched it. She stroked the dog's back and told him Jeremiah would be home soon, but her words had little effect that she could see in his eyes.

John thought to reassure Katherine. "Take heart, dear Katherine. Jeremiah will be home," he said. He felt in his heart it was to be true.

Chapter 17

Harris listened along with a small group of lieutenants to Ostam rant about the imminent invasion of his throne. He was now the senior army officer and in line to step up to the court soon. The leader was furious and was planning the defense of his power. The interloper had to be captured before he made it to Carolina. "That bunch of southern murderers has stolen from us! They have come here, killed Gack, invaded our house, and taken our people. We cannot let this pass! You must stop them! It has to be that damned Carolina swarm of pests! Don't bring any of them back. Kill them all! You must then root out every last under who murdered Raymond and Dobey! You all know what to do and do not return to me until this hive of insects has been wiped out like they should have been in the fires!"

"Move now, you men! Follow me!" Harris commanded when Ostam finished and turned his back on the crowd.

Harris was confident because of the army's easy kills in Houston and good results; he was sure this mission would be little different. The enemy had guns but weren't the army of Baltimore. These mountain people have now invited a reckoning, he thought. It doesn't matter how many there are; the enemy will soon be dead. He struck out with nearly the entire army behind him and headed south at full speed, leaving only a garrison of one hundred men behind to guard Baltimore. He was the General, the man who gave the orders, the one who would enforce Ostam's charge without question and without mercy. It was the largest force ever sent out on an expedition and included over four hundred armed soldiers.

The sight was a wave of lights penetrating the darkness and turning the road in front of the army into an illuminated sea of hundreds of twin specks moving desperately. Bunched together and rolling toward a yet unseen target, the purpose was to capture and kill the renegades rather than allow them success.

Throwing away the bonds of the only true government in the country was a capital offense. Such an affront motivated Harris more than any single issue did, more than any single man could. His life and career were tied directly to the system Ostam created.

He led them south, racing to take Jeremiah, though he did not know him or the fact that he was a lone warrior. He didn't know where the thief was taking his bounty. He did know what he had done. His advantage in catching him was speed. He had his column pour it on and was moving the largest army Ostam had ever sent into battle very fast. Harris was now Ostam's second-in-command and led his portion of the army along the same path Morford had taken. The four hundred-man army included the most recent volunteers and conscripts who had no training but were quickly put into uniform and thrown to Harris as numbers, not as professionals.

Every male of the under-ghetto over fourteen years old was put into the force. Some knew nothing of freedom. Many had heard of liberty in their dimly lit shelters where under-fathers whispered its meaning and virtues to give their sons and daughters hope. Teaching it fed the fathers' need for a little light in the darkness that was now Baltimore.

Jeremiah turned back and saw a tiny flash behind them. He had to watch the dark road in front with just enough moonlight to make out the edges of the road ahead. He glanced back again. Now he was sure he saw something—more than one flicker. That meant one thing and one thing only. The enemy was on the chase.

John felt a sudden deep worry but knew that evil had not yet swallowed Jeremiah—of that, he was certain. He called a council session quickly. "Please come together in our lodge, ladies and gentlemen... we must pray together for the safe return of our neighbor, our friend, Jeremiah."

The fuel would be gone soon. The enemy guessed right. Harris was bearing down on the small group who could do the state no harm. Jeremiah had to protect the ten hearts he rescued over the next one hundred miles south by southwest to the mountains of his people.

He knew the countryside and how to forage and survive. He would teach them and make it to western Carolina, make it to Katherine, return to Jack the dog, and his village. He slowed the car to fix his sight on the landscape to his right as best he could to make it out through the blackness.

Jeremiah knew he was well past the old town of Blacksburg and near old Winston-Salem when he finally saw a rise in the land well off the road. It was dim, darkened off to the right—and probably wooded—that would give him a chance if he could make it into a curtain of trees and move his charge to safety.

He turned the car off the road and watched as the fourteen-year-old followed him into the unknown, trusting and scared as he was. The field off the road was rough and filled with unseen depressions and rocks that the night shielded from sight, even with the beams shining from the car. He drove on, through a weak fence, jarring his passengers and wrecking the car as it bottomed out, skipping across the field. He punched the gas and alternately let off as he ran into and across obstacles and ditches, over things left long ago, and through the grasses just starting to thrive again.

The lights behind him were more numerous now and bearing closer. He stopped when he ran into a steep cut of earth that had been there for years. The ravine would hide them from the enemy for a little while. He jumped out and ran to the car behind him.

"Get out! We must move on foot from here! Everyone, come with me, quickly! We must make it to the trees… Now, run!" Jeremiah commanded, his voice pushing energy through the young bodies such that there was no doubt about the urgency inside each of the ten who were willing to take a chance with this stranger.

The cars were left over one hundred yards from the old Interstate and sank into the landscape as everything else did over time, becoming merely another collection of trash left by the nation's few living inhabitants after the great fires. Jeremiah knew that if they were going to be lucky, the cars would not be seen as the hoard passed below. If they were not, the children could be captured and returned to Baal.

He led them into the trees and quickly to the south, taking the slope gently by moving through the trees and across, moving slightly upward with each several steps he took. The air was cool and rapidly turning cold. The dark forest made it worse. It began to feel even colder as the night grew longer. Jeremiah knew he had to find them shelter soon. There were bound to be old abandoned houses nearby, some nearly destroyed but still offering shelter. Many still had some structure.

Inside the lodge of the mountain tribe near old Asheville, John felt his spiritual heart growing, building. He received a vision and knew what he should do as the Chief. One warrior was out in the country, making his way back home. That warrior needed more from the tribe now to complete his mission.

"We shall move north to receive Jeremiah. Many may be after him even now. Of that, I'm not certain, but still, we should prepare for him! For all those who will do the work once again, prepare for a journey of days so that we may find our brave citizen. We must be light and able to move quickly."

Jeremiah led the children on a trek over six miles, reaching the summit of a hill with them before stopping. He looked back and didn't see anything toward the road. He found a high point and turned to see what was happening on the road they had just left. The army chasing them was nowhere in sight, but he knew the horizon at that distance could be hiding them. He thought they might be safe for a time and could find some shelter near the shallow forest. Once, there had been plenty of houses along the road for miles at a stretch. He was sure he would see one if he walked further into the dark.

"Is everyone doing all right?" he asked the ten. "Is anyone hurting?"

"I believe we're all okay, mister," Mary's son answered after looking around at the others.

"We need to move quickly then and find a house to get out of this cold."

"We're ready. It's better to walk than to stay here," the boy replied, beginning to lose his fear of adults and coming out of the forced silence he had grown accustomed to with Gack.

"What is your name, son? What are all your names?" Jeremiah asked their lost faces to assure them of their safety. Time was now an ally. He knew they had escaped the hell of Baal.

"I'm Matthew, sir," Mary's son was the first to speak. "There are some here who don't know a name other than what Gack told them. They have been in his house for so long—they were too small when he took them to remember anything of their parents."

Jeremiah lowered his head in shame for what other adults had done there. There are cruel men and women who live like animals, with far more cunning than any animal and far less heart than any animal. They prey on children such as these—and anyone who would stop them from taking others' love and hope and smashing it all for the sake of their own minds, their own warped, terrible minds, he thought. How many innocents are still there? God help us save them all, he prayed silently.

He took them down the back slope of the hill to find shelter. Just short of a mile from where they started, he could make out the outline of structures. He turned them toward an overgrown path and stepped over a large fallen tree, its trunk soft and rotting. There was a possible shelter within sight. The young people with him followed closely in his footsteps.

They reached an open space near the house, and Jeremiah could see that it might work well as shelter for all of them. It was a large house and appeared to be intact. At one time, it must have been home to a fairly well-to-do family. The façade was one of those two-story places built in the nineties, with its stone and brick front framing a large portal window on its second floor. He opened the door to the spacious foyer that centered a few rooms at ground level, and in the far wall of the room, there was an intact set of stairs that led to rooms upstairs. Jeremiah detected the odor of burnt wood still lingering in the air inside the house. The back of the house showed severe fire damage, but most of it still stood as a deteriorating piece of evidence of a destroyed neighborhood. This was one of tens of thousands of neighborhoods in the past where once the children played outside and around neatly trimmed shrubs and under healthy trees.

An odd accumulation of trash was left in the foyer, piled in a heap that rested against one side more prominently than against the other walls.

Torn and damaged furniture pieces were strewn here and there, obviously no longer arranged. They had been used over the years by some passers-by who survived and were seeking new homes as he had when he found the village. Jeremiah thought it likely that some of them found themselves in Baltimore while most of them died along the way.

"Matthew and I will check the area first, but we will stay here until morning. Stay close to me until we make sure it is safe."

He started inspecting the house as best he could in the dark for any creatures and dangerous objects that might injure the children. The air was stale from years of abandonment. The kitchen area was complete with all the appliances, though rusted in places, doors opened and left to hang until the hinges gave way. The oven, refrigerator, and most of the cabinets were left as scavengers took what they could for food.

There were still plates and silverware, now mostly broken or bent. He was able to see each item he picked up by holding samples up to a window and using the stars and moon glow through the glass. Rust clung to several spoons and forks like infected little things no longer useful. He saw there were pictures left in one corner and stooped to see them. The family who lived here included a man, woman, and three children of school age. Their faces and ages were frozen at this point in their lives prior to the bad days. The picture was now something left as refuse inside an empty house.

He thought of his mother and father and how very blessed he was that they taught him and happened to live in a space that escaped most of the fires. These parents probably taught theirs too, and they are somewhere safe, I pray, he thought as he replaced the photographs back where he found them.

He and Matthew went through every room and listened for movement. There was none. Jeremiah returned to the group waiting in the center of the foyer and told them this place would do for a rest. "Stay together. I have these for you to use as covers," he said as he handed out a collection of a tablecloth, old sheets, towels, one holey tarpaulin he found, and a few garments left in the place. "Rest easy now, young people… In the morning, we walk."

Harris and the army screamed to the Virginia-North Carolina line and then went right another one hundred miles on old Interstate 40 following the faintest light—barely a speck ahead of them—and then the light was gone. He knew they had to be close. It was time to plan and move on the escapees and anyone who was attempting to hide them. Ostam's words about a force near here could not be a deterrent or a worry —he had four hundred soldiers. That should be plenty to wipe the opposition out, he figured. There is no one as powerful as Ostam and no one more capable of taking care of the leader's business than he.

"No fires. Move everyone off the road," he commanded. Morford had been here before and knew they were close too, but had many miles still to travel. He nervously moved his sleep blanket off the road, looking ahead down the road toward the pit that took Dobey. Inexplicably, he felt sweat seeping out of every pore across his skin into the cold.

Harris was out of fuel except for reserves to return. From this point on the southern earth, the army would be on foot. Much as armies had traveled before, he would follow the same path to conquer. The mountains loomed ahead at a great distance. In the twilight, he could make out the soft outlines of the range of long-running humps to the south. It was there he would lead his army to find their prey and triumph.

"Lieutenant, we'll turn west and head toward the mountains. That is where we'll find them. I say we stay on the road and keep moving until we reach them tomorrow."

"Very well, Captain," he said. "Do you think the stories are true?"

"No. We're four hundred strong. No one alive can beat us! We'll find the runaways and the killer—all the killers—and separate their heads from their bodies, every one of them! Ostam is waiting!"

John and the villagers gathered for the most important council meeting. The mood was solemn. Katherine began to cry. The crowd pushed toward John, the Chief.

"I tell you now, brave people, our brother has been on a great journey and is close. He struck out alone to find Mary's son as the best chance to free him. This single heart full of love that ties people of goodwill to one another—the love that sets people free—took the challenge and met it. I have felt it mightily.

It has come to us now, as surely the forces who would stop him do not know love, do not know what it is to be free, to meet him. We must stop those who would take him and protect him at the end of his brave journey!

I know it is true an enemy comes. Whether it is one hundred or one thousand, we must meet them and take Jeremiah into the protection of our hearts as he has taken Mary's son into his. He is risking every breath he may yet take to save him! Though not a single breath is promised, I know this much too—Jeremiah has many to take with his bride, Katherine.

Let us remember our ancestors and remember what it is to be a warrior—that despite what lies before us and how many there are who wish to kill us—we will stand strong! We must stand for our people, our life; our nation… for no one has the right to take from us that which we cannot give—our liberty!

In the Lord's name, and if it be God's will, we shall have victory! He already knows the outcome, and we are but those who see and know Him. May God be with us! We're not going to them to start a mortal fight. We're going to them to finish the fight! Come with me now! Let's move together and show them nothing can prevail against an army of free people!"

John picked up his rifle and silently walked out of the lodge. Men and women took up their arms and followed. No words were spoken among them as they quietly followed him. The village turned out, leaving some behind to tend to the children—those who were asked to stay knew their job was to remain behind without protest. The children were quiet and seemed to know it wasn't the time to be restless. Solemnly, the people split into groups and set to do their job.

The dawn of that day brought light and fresh air. Jeremiah breathed it in deeply and felt the touch of the first few rays of sunshine begin to warm his face. He shook his head to wake up completely and surveyed their surroundings now that he could see them more clearly. There was no sign of them. The scene reminded him of a better, happier time. The destruction had not been as complete in this area of Carolina, and for an instant, he thought this might be what life is like in the country. The only thing missing was its people moving about. He and the children were the only ones using the space now.

The roadways nearby appeared to be clear. The hills behind him and the fields in front of him appeared clean and green, though overgrown.

There were trees showing signs of early spring life and blooming. He heard birds and saw some flying here and there, around the structures and trees. He took in the sweetness of an innocent land—the kind of innocence and life that fills a man with hope and good cheer. He saw the blue sky punctuated by white streaks of soft, long clouds that were peaceful and beautiful. Nothing was threatening; all of it welcomed them in the sweet embrace of nature.

The children followed him in line as they began the trek across the countryside toward the mountains of the Americans. Matthew took up a makeshift pack of food and blankets. He carried more than he could use. Other children who were strong enough did the same.

Jeremiah knew they might cross the path of the people who were looking for them. His chance to be successful depended on his ability to see them first and avoid contact. He took his pistol out first and checked it. He then checked the rifle to make sure it was ready too in case he would need it. They were steadily walking and nearing home.

Harris moved his army on the road that swallowed Dobey and Raymond. He had the large force of four hundred men behind him, walking on both sides of the asphalt in long lines that stretched a mile. He was not sure how far they had to go to find the spy and his haul of Ostam's property. He marched in long strides and expected every one of the four hundred to stay with him. Those who were toward the back of the lines had to step up and run between several steps in order to catch up to the front. Many were moving while showing the first signs of exhaustion. The army tried to keep their formation tight and avoid getting too far behind.

Chapter 18

Of all the towering peaks and deep valleys of a life, Jeremiah had touched nearly every kind. None of that bothered him, nor was his experience worth even a bit of regret. He saw the light of a new day for him, Katherine, and Jack. He would find food and water for the children —the precious gifts who were now precious members of the tribe. On this, I promise! Not a single hair on their heads will be taken past me; only over me shall evil take these lives again!

Putting miles behind them, Jeremiah heard no complaints, no whining from them. They were a serious group, more mature than their years accounted for. He might have expected some of them to cry with aches or worry, and he could soothe the child as best he could. Each child in the group was earnest and determined now, less of a child and more of a mature human being seeking liberty, just smaller. He became more sure of this group as time passed and loved them for their hearts and determination. They were strong. He smiled broadly with pride. He thought of them and how brave they remained after all they had been through in their young lives. Our youth are amazing people, he thought. They were nearing old Asheville and planned to stop there to give them rest for a time before making it to the mountains and taking the three steep slopes in one day. He knew that would test the limits of each young one's endurance.

Harris's columns were moving into Asheville, a quiet, still city that now gave way to shadows and ghostly evidence of the past. A common scene, the deserted streets filled with old vehicle hulks and heaps of wood, steel, and all manner of trash that did not burn, left as it fell or as the wind moved it. There were skeletons of animals, people, and buildings left as a result—the outcome of hate, the product of greed, when respect for others was absent in the minds of those who had triggers. These places, and what caused them to be as they were now, remained dark evidence of the truth that destiny was sharp and used its full force.

He marched his army through her center, encountering no one, only the dust left from a past that led a nation—and all nations—to the end of their circle, their profound rise and complete fall. Left to scavenge were few people—some like Ostam and some like Jeremiah. Both worked toward a restoration. Their vision differed only because of what was inside them, what they believed in with their whole being.

"How's everyone doing?" Jeremiah asked his group.

"I see they're hungry, mister," Matthew said. "Can we find them something to eat and some water?"

"Yes, I will, Matthew. Let's make it to the trees ahead and stop. That's where we can find food. Asheville is only about ten miles away, so we can take some time."

He hoped there would at least be wineberry blooms near the forest range, along with edible acorns, and knew there would be pine needles he could gather as a last resort for the children to eat. He figured the only water to be found would come from a stream or a dig with his long knife. If he could find some, there might be snakes, squirrels, or even fish to prepare on a flat rock over a small fire. He slowed the pace and led them toward the tree line.

With blankets and towels draped over their shoulders, the young people followed him, appearing as a line of old-time Christian monks. Their faces were framed by the cloths they wore and the slings fashioned to carry their coverings easily. Only Matthew had grown to within inches of Jeremiah's height and had yet to finish growing. The slow march of Jeremiah and his small band of followers continued deeper into the forest's protection.

At the same time, Harris placed several men ahead of him as they began to pass through Asheville. "Be watchful. Shout out if you see anything move!" he commanded as he sank toward the center of the long column for safety.

John was in front of the Americans. He moved as if gliding across the landscape, alongside every member of the village who came with him. The army of the people was a wave of fighters coming to meet the enemy. With every step, there was no hesitation—only determination in every heart on the march. John held the flag unfurled as a sign to heaven that he knew God, understood his faith, and that their cause was protected. The bearer felt it a special privilege that he accepted humbly.

Sunlight danced off rifle barrels with every step as hundreds of men and women carried their tools for when they were needed. It was only a matter of time before the village would once again be tested. There were no smiles, no talking as the wave moved to the road to confront the enemy who would kill Jeremiah if they caught him. They would stop them without remorse or second thought. There would be no hesitation to enter this destiny either.

Katherine and Mary were among them, each carrying a weapon like every other warrior in the army. Katherine wanted Jeremiah back. Mary wanted her son Matthew back. Both kept their eyes fixed forward for any sign and followed their flag. Both touched the trigger guard and slid their hands to feel the trigger. Both were ready to do their part when the time came.

The village wave rolled toward Asheville. The mass of people came to find Jeremiah and the boy and protect them. John waved to the crowd to use the available cover as they walked onward. Jack the dog was excited, as if he sensed his master was close and could detect his scent. Near the outskirts of the city, the wave stopped and took positions to form a firm and strong wall. John led a few scouts out of their fortress.

Jeremiah placed the flat rock onto the fire. He gave it time to heat and laid the squirrel and snake fillets across its surface. The children waited, munched on the few berries they found, and carefully sipped on the water. He showed them how to strain the water he collected from the ground. Matthew used the long knife to dig into the earth for enough to quench their thirst. Jeremiah knew those who hunted them could be nearby, and they needed to finish eating and move.

"Tear it off with your teeth," he said to a young girl who was unsure how to eat the jagged-looking meat slice. "It's good for you. Go ahead," he smiled.

He scanned the horizon and kept watch for any strangers while the children finished their modest meal. He stamped the fire out and covered it with dirt and small stones. "We must go," he said quietly to them. "We'll be home soon."

He took them deeper into the forest—a better place to hide from anyone they did not want to find them. Jeremiah also knew the forest allowed him to approach the enemy at any moment without warning. He led them through young pines and hulks of old dead oaks, stepping over the thick floor of rotting wood and new growth that covered the layer of ash. He took them up a hill that emerged covered with seedlings among the remnants of trees lying all around, nearly blocking every step they took. Suddenly, he stopped the ten and whispered for them to remain quiet and still.

The crest of the hill offered little cover. The growth was just beginning to recover, and the highest point at the top was still clear and open. He turned away and instead took them across the slope still hidden by the forest.

Another hour passed as they worked across the land. Jeremiah saw the end of the forest just ahead. He studied the fields he could make out far outside the sudden border to their south and west. He went to the edge where he stooped low to get a better look. He saw many foundations of houses—neighborhoods that appeared as man-made attempts to challenge nature, leveled by tornadoes. There were cracked asphalt streets bordered by overgrown stalks, weeds, and other grasses. Wreckage of cars, trucks, and human desperation left dirty evidence that he had once been here in all his vanity. Throughout the roads and to the end of each cul-de-sac, the sad vision remained as the story of innocence caught up in a man-induced hell because of its indifference. It was a familiar scene to every survivor these days. It's the kind of playground now that must delight Ostam, he thought.

Jeremiah looked out and away toward the south for another hour, remaining hidden and still. He saw something moving on the distant horizon and stayed fixed on the slight ripple he could see. It wasn't getting larger, but it did seem to be moving to his left until he could see it no more. They were somewhere near or in the city, stalking prey, and hunting deep in the center of the city, he thought. It has to be them! They're close, and we have to get around them to our mountains. Lord help me. Lord be with us and guide us… please. Lord, thank you for everything, he prayed silently.

John saw them first. He counted as many as he could see while watching from behind a stone pillar that once was the base of a bronze statue—now long missing, probably destroyed by the last of the scavengers who bartered the metal for something they wanted. Two warriors waited with him behind the same carved pillar, remaining out of sight. "I see them. There are many."

Hours passed, and dusk arrived. It would be dark soon, making it more difficult to watch their movements. John returned to the warrior army who waited. Their stoic and strong presence was a normal understanding. He had them take turns sleeping and watching. He took up the flag and left their lines. He walked toward the enemy camp in the dark and approached within two hundred yards, where he placed the flag upright and centered it on the street. It was positioned in the open as a warning to the Baltimore army to return from where they came and come no further into this valley. The words embroidered on the fabric that symbolized Americans were used long ago in the hard, bloody past of the birth of the once great nation. The art of a coiled snake gave warning. John returned to his people to wait for their response.

The Americans moved closer that night and took up their positions in a quarter-moon curve facing the enemy encampment to wait.

Harris believed in his master Ostam with all that was inside his body and mind. He accepted the lies as necessary tools to control a scared population. He thought he knew what was best for the people, almost as much as Ostam himself. He knew that following him would guarantee his success and happiness. He would destroy the people who dared to trespass Baal, kill them, and take all they had for Ostam. He was confident the battle would be his and that he would root out the evil of such people. He would ravage the den of killers in the mountains and return with one survivor, Mary, the killer. He would take every child that was forced to come to this place, and then take his place next to the great leader. He smiled widely just before going to sleep. What glory awaits me! I'll have it all!

James was to teach mathematics and physics to a select group of people. Ostam wanted them to be productive technicians to service lights and heat in the main hall and engineer methods of food production and meat harvesting. An order came down to him as a matter of survival that he follow the directive and produce results with these strangers. It took James little time to understand what was happening in this city. Rather than acting with free will, it was forced work. Free will had been taken away daily as any food might be by some and this Ostam fellow. He's their leader and their law, James thought. Ostam is another Hitler of old.

Ostam kept a few armed guards close to him for his protection. James didn't know how many there were or the strength of his army—nor did he know most had left for Carolina. He knew Julie was supposed to work on the generators and had been taken away soon after their arrival. They had grown close during the lonely years, and he missed her company. He worried about her welfare more than her absence. I have to find her, he thought.

He worked to clear a large room and arrange the chairs and desks needed for the ten-hour days of instruction he was ordered to provide. He was under the watchful gaze of a single guard who didn't hesitate to point a rifle toward him. Once a day, he was given a piece of pig meat and a cup of water for his meal. There was just enough to sustain life, provided daily when the Baal government employed you.

Suddenly, he heard noises outside the room. It sounded like a struggle of some kind, punctuated by shouting and heavy footsteps in the corridor outside his space. He turned just as a group of soldiers passed the open door and saw a man being wrestled and forced by three men down the hallway. He was bloodied, and so were the men who were forcing him to go with them. He was fighting them every step of the way. It was Lee, the old mechanic.

The guard assigned to James and the classroom quickly moved toward the struggle to assist the others handling the man, now only a wild bear—a beast who was not compliant. James beat the guard to the door to help Lee. As soon as he took a step to aid his friend, he was struck from above, fell to his knees, and then rolled unconscious to the floor. Blood flowed brightly from his head in a thin, steady stream across the yellow tile. He'd been struck with a rifle butt he never saw coming from behind him. He woke up barely conscious, his eyes unfocused.

Julie… where are you, dear heart, dear woman? I see you walking through the yellow and green fields, the sunlight gracing your skin and hair, and the smile that is you—on you. You fill my heart and raise my spirits in this awful place, this painful world we now have after all we could do to finish her. Come to me, sweetness. Let me hold you close to my heart and feel your life in me too. I love you, Julie.

He woke up fully and felt wetness all across his head and into his neck where the guards had dumped a bucket of rancid water to revive him. He felt the painful area on his skull and brought a weak hand to it to press, massage, and soothe the wound. He could see enough through the cloudy vision remaining in his mind to know he was still in a foreign place and nowhere near a field of wildflowers or sunny skies.

He felt a sudden lift by intrusive arms that brought him to his feet. Gone was Lee, taken away to some other place. He thought his friend must be confined further away in the building. James managed to form a thought about the old man soon after regaining consciousness. "What happened to Lee? Where is he?" he asked the group of guards around him. He felt a hard slap against his cheek. There was no answer.

"Let me be clear, teacher! You people are to obey! You're not to show any aggression," one of them said. The guards had finally spoken to him without striking him or knocking him out. "You must get back to work."

He longed for the life they had in Indianapolis. At the sight of the guns, they had no choice but to surrender. He knew they were imprisoned for no crime other than simply existing. Whether they would ever be free again was the question. How, he thought. How can we escape this place and return home? How can we live as we once did?

He watched and waited until the guards fell asleep. It was 1:00 AM. James rose from the pallet allotted to him in the small room next to his classroom. Carefully, he moved to the door and felt the latch turn. It was not locked. Turning the hardware slowly, he eased the door open slightly and waited, listening for any sign of a guard nearby. He slowly eased the door open to see the hallway.

Since the day of their arrival, they had all been separated once Ostam assigned their work. He had not seen Julie, but he did see Lee the day before as the man was dragged through this particular corridor. He thought that might mean Julie was close. Maybe all of them are close, he thought.

He slipped outside into the hallway. Passing the door to his work, he gazed at his prison and quickly turned his eyes back to the long hall. The building was massive. There were many doors—and he was only on one wing on the second floor of what must be at least a ten-story government palace.

He didn't know where to begin to look for Lee, Julie, or anyone else from Indianapolis. We should have been ready to fight, he thought. It was too late now.

I'm James McAlister. I teach. I like to garden herbs and spices. I enjoy a good meal from simple things, from fish to lentils, to soups of tomato, beans, and anything healthful I can swallow. I love teaching and watching my students grasp the material from the simple to the complex! To see them achieve understanding means everything, knowing that doing so will help them create and enjoy a better life!

I'm a free man despite the bondage others have placed on my physical body! I've done nothing to deserve this degradation as a prisoner here or anywhere! These people have no right to keep me or force me to serve them! That is what they're doing. The people with the guns are taking slaves for themselves. The gun makes the difference. It's in the wrong hands, wrong minds, and wrong hearts—just wrong.

This is what our nation has come to. We let it happen because we didn't think it would. We didn't think it could. Our arrogance led us to a war that killed most of the people. We allowed these kinds of people to become what they are! It is our fault, and our lives are at stake now—for what they are. We sat down and wallowed in indifference, and now this is what we nourished, but the evil is not in all minds, thank God!

If we had been in greater numbers with greater courage, maybe we could have held the foolish governments back and turned them out. If we had done that, this earth would not have become what it is now, after so many died so horribly—as the tragedy of man's sure end because of man's failures. It was certain! If we had only thought to be prepared—

those of us who still lived in peaceful character when it comes to others—but we didn't. We didn't know how many others came through the nuclear war and should not have been so narrow-minded that we hardly considered others who also survived as we did and what they were like. I miss my family and friends. For reasons I don't know, I didn't join them when I should have. I was supposed to die with them and did not.

All he could do was try every door and get as far as he could before being stopped and discovered outside his room where he was told to remain when he was not at work. Lee was brought this way. They took him down this hall several steps before I was hit. He decided to begin trying the doors toward the end of the hallway to find Lee.

Chapter 19

Armies Collide

Dawn broke earlier, and the air was warmer. Harris wiped the sleep away with his hand. This will be the day! he thought as he stood and stretched, like a preening peacock spreading its feathers in a show of color and length to attract a female. For the time and the occasion, he took on the mantle of the great leader. He had four hundred men and many weak lieutenants who would kill for him. He felt he had all the power in the world and was now ready to use it. No one could possibly stop him, the invincible Harris!

The rush startled him. Suddenly, an unknown man—one of the nameless soldiers—was pushed toward him. A lieutenant brought a solitary man to his quarters who appeared to be out of breath and scared.

"What is this?" Harris bellowed angrily.

"Someone was putting a flag up there, sir," the soldier said, pointing in the direction of the army's planned movement.

"Someone? What does that mean, Lieutenant? What is this man talking about?"

"There's a flag or banner put on the road that wasn't there last night, sir."

"You're telling me that a stranger came that close to us? You're telling me that the sentry didn't see or hear something? That's outrageous! He'll be shot for this! Bring me the man who was on duty near there and make it quick!"

"But, sir… What about the flag?" the lieutenant said.

"So they're playing with us? We're going to kill them all anyway. I don't care about any flag. It means nothing. They'll still die—and that will happen today! Understood?" Let them think they intimidate us—it won't work, he thought as he reached for the rifle leaned nearby and clutched its stock, a dear feel to him.

The villagers waited in line and watched from cover.

Jeremiah knew there were a large number of Ostam's soldiers looking for him who were moving through Asheville. He had to avoid them and take the children around the old shell of a city to reach the tribe's mountains. That meant miles of a wide arch well out of sight. It was the only way.

"It's quiet here," Harris said to his lieutenant, stirring next to him after the errant sentry was brought to his makeshift camp headquarters. After dispatching two of his soldiers to shoot the sleeper in the back of his neck for dereliction of duty in the presence of his army, he planned to make his move toward the mountains. "All we've seen is a silly flag. No one stayed to fight," he said with a smirk and began to laugh. "All this fuss is over nothing! Ostam shouldn't worry about these cowards. We'll be in their camp before night. It'll be our camp."

"It's very quiet, Captain. They're all hiding. This'll be easy—not even as hard as Houston or Indianapolis."

"Very well, Lieutenant. Set the army ready to move out within ten minutes. I'll take the front."

Harris walked in front of an army divided on either side of the road, each side a long line of armed men. His brisk pace set the confident awareness he expected every soldier under his command to know at this hour of triumph.

Jeremiah and the children made their way south of Asheville and turned more north and west several miles outside the old city limits. The only animals they disturbed were a variety of birds and a few rabbits that quickly jumped and ran away from the small troop. He used the dead reckoning of the early sun's position to navigate the countryside well away from those who were in Asheville.

"What is that?" Harris closed in quickly toward the lieutenant. "Do you see them?"

Harris raised his arm to stop the columns behind him. "I see them. That's where the flag came from, and here they are, offering themselves up to us," he said and smiled.

Distant figures stood in place well ahead of the army bearing down on them. Three blurs rose from the road and were still.

"Go with me, Lieutenant. Let's see who they are," the captain said as he lowered his rifle to ready and quickly stepped forward. The figures did not move and waited for him.

"Yes, sir," he said as he motioned a squad of thirteen to join them while the rest of the army waited behind.

"Put the men on both sides of the road, Lieutenant," the captain ordered and turned toward them. "Be ready to shoot them when I give the order!"

"They're still there, Captain."

"Yeah—let them stand and meet us up close," he said and laughed. "They won't live to regret their game!"

The march continued, and they did not see the three figures move or run away. After thirty minutes of a quick step, the figures were nowhere to be seen.

"What the hell, Lieutenant? Where did they go?" Harris asked his second-in-command.

"I don't know, sir. I didn't see them move anywhere!"

"You sound nervous! Never show hesitation, Lieutenant! That'll give the enemy an edge. Do you understand? They must have ducked away. They have to be close," he said as he looked to both sides of the road for hiding places. There seemed to be very few, as the landscape was mostly barren except for a few distant skeletons of buildings, probably barns and such—and most were well off the road. They must be lying down around here, he thought.

"Lieutenant, get your people off the road now!" he said, fearing an ambush although an ambush meant suicide for the attackers. If they were pinned down, the large number of men behind them would take care of any provocation like that.

Suddenly, a voice called out to them. "Who are you?"

Harris looked at his lieutenant. "Where did that come from? Did you hear it?"

"Yes, sir—I heard it. I believe it came from our left."

"We are the army of Baal," Harris first shouted toward the left and then repeated toward the right side of the road. "Who are you?"

"I am John, the Chief of the American people."

"Chief? Well then, tell me, Chief, why are you harboring a murderer? We have come here for one who calls herself Mary. We demand that if you have her, you turn her over to us. Do you understand?" The disdain in his voice was clear in the tone and manner he spoke.

"Why are so many seeking one woman?" a voice said clearly.

"Show yourself! I won't be talking to air! Come out of your hole, Chief, so I can see you!"

"Foolish man, I'm in the wind before you now. We do not keep a murderer here and tell you now to leave and return to where you came from."

Harris laughed at the voice's impertinence and fairy tale talk of being part of the wind as such nonsense. He'll die soon along with his people, he thought.

"We'll not go anywhere except into that mountain where you're keeping her! I tell you now that if you don't help us and submit, you and your people will be destroyed! Do you not see how many we are to your very few?"

The voice held silent. Harris stooped down behind cover in anticipation of an attack. Minute after minute passed. Harris figured the so-called Chief was counting his few options—and would decide that his only option for safety would cause him to yield the road any minute. Regardless, Harris planned to kill them all. The captain couldn't wait any longer.

"Answer me, coward! Come out and give up your arms—you know what I'm talking about—the ones you used to kill our people who came before! I know all about it, Chief," he said, squeezing the word "chief" between his lips in utter contempt and impatience.

The deep, unwavering voice of John suddenly resonated throughout the earth on both sides of the road and filled the unwanted visitor's ears. "No. We shall not comply! Let this be your warning. Turn and leave in peace or be destroyed. I tell you now; you leave us now or not see another sunrise."

What is this silly talk about not complying? Who do they think they are—just who in the hell do they think they are… this not complying… crazy, stupid,

sentiment, a crazy way to think! They're all going to die! Harris thought. He barely had the self-discipline to wait until his army could attack to carry out the deed.

John's voice rang out again. "Know this: We do not desire to kill. We will kill all of you. Be warned. Do not doubt that, strangers."

"You're going to kill us all by yourself, with maybe a few others? You're hiding in the weeds and threatening this army? You're a fool, sir."

"Take my words as truth. Heed them, stranger, for you have entered a free America."

"I understand nothing you say. It is nothing more than a silly bluff! We are many and strong. We will destroy you and all your people! You must give way and comply with our demands! I'm not talking anymore."

Harris waved to the Lieutenant and the men crouched just off the sides of the road. "Let's go. There's nothing here."

Harris sat down on dead leaves and waited for his army to form a line of attack. He would kill them all, including Mary, and report to Ostam that she was in the enemy's lines and couldn't be spared because of the cover they took in the forest.

On the way back to the rest of his army, Harris did not say anything or allow his Lieutenant to speak. He knew that after moving a distance away from the flag, he would not be overheard. Once he returned to the rest of his army, he gave the Lieutenant the plan. They were going to move the army in a large curved blade shape to sweep over the area and eliminate anyone they found hiding.

"They're nothing more than little cowards hiding from me. They won't last long," he finished, his confident smirk signaling to the Lieutenants how certain he was of being in those mountains before dusk. "Begin moving, Lieutenant."

The army moved toward the relatively flat area, spread wide in a line, toward the place where the flag was staked in the center of the road.

It was a hunt-and-destroy mission. Harris marched forward behind his army.

The village warriors had become the grasses and waited. No soldier in Harris's army could see anyone to fire at as they stepped closer and closer. The Americans waited until the line was near them, within yards. The warriors were patient and unafraid. Not a single shot was fired early in the long minutes the enemy approached. Not a sound gave them away as the trap remained set and ready. The noisy army walked toward the defenders as part of another ordinary day for them.

Expecting three criminals hiding nearby—maybe a few more who did not show themselves—Harris knew he would surely find them soon. He smiled with anticipation of finding them and visiting his form of retribution on the arrogant bastards cowering in weeds and trash—the trash they were to him.

He walked well behind the front lines formed by the conscripted unders and others who simply enjoyed having a job that placed them into a position of some power. It will happen soon, he thought. His soldiers would see anyone jumping up from the grasses, trying to run away. A matter of time, and this city will be mine, and then on to that mountain hideout.

Jeremiah could see the mountains, though the ridges were still at a good distance. He figured they had roughly twenty miles to go before he would reach the three ridges of the spine that was home. The children seemed to be doing well and making the journey with him in good spirits and health. He looked back at each one of them and made sure—as best as he could—that each was able to keep the pace steady and unencumbered.

Within the bowels of Baal, James slowly opened his eyes. He realized his left arm was suspended well over his head and tightly tied to the ceiling. He felt pain in his shoulder radiating down the entire length of his arm. He could barely see through the swollen tissue beneath each eye and quickly knew he had been beaten. His lips were cut and sore. He was able to make out bloodstains that crossed over his chin and down his neck, painting a spread of branches along the neckline. He had failed.

The guards found him and beat him again. He didn't know if it was still night or day. He knew he couldn't move and was defenseless in their hands. He focused his eyes and studied the room as best he could, unable to turn his body much to either side. He noticed a body clumped over itself in the corner. It was bent over legs and feet and not moving. A covering had been thrown carelessly over the head, but he could see a bloody hand stretching out from the dark cloth lying motionless next to the body's leg. It appeared to be the size of Lee's arms—stocky and strong. It's probably Lee, and he looks like he's dead.

He cried. Lee wouldn't leave his mind. Julie wouldn't leave his mind, nor did he want her to go. He knew his time might very well be over soon as he was likely to meet the same end as the old mechanic. He had no choice but to wait for what they would do to him next in this place of horror. Yes, we should have been prepared to fight for at least a chance, and now we have no chance.

Suddenly a flag appeared again, seen by the soldiers moving across the fields toward the center of town. Harris heard a stir ahead and called out to his Lieutenant. "What is it? Why have they stopped? I didn't order them to stop!" he shouted, beginning to curse them.

"Captain Harris, that flag has been raised again! It came out of nowhere, and our soldiers are uneasy."

"Push on, I tell you! Damn, man, get them moving!"

In an instant, humps of grass rose as one body and leveled hot lead into the bodies of several soldiers who fell nearly in the same short window of time. At the same instant, more than one hundred took their last breath in the first volley from the villagers as those living nervously fired wildly. The noise rose to a pitch that was deafening, frightening Harris, causing waves of nerves to course through his body as he fell for cover, quivering, reeling, and quickly speechless. He could open his mouth but was not able to make words come out.

The Americans fired from the arch they had formed and set the invaders into the center of the deadly intersection where streaks of death cut them down. Another one hundred fell as the survivors who remained standing dropped to the ground to hide. Most dropped their weapons and tried to become part of the earth to escape certain death.

Most of the strangers failed to react quickly enough. Harris quickly lost his army to unseen defenders who used tactics as old as those used in the wars that shaped the earth into the place it was now. There was no mercy, no quarter, as one by one the few survivors left from Baal were destroyed, except those who fell to hide in the grasses. Those few included Harris, now showing his cowardice.

The warriors cut them down in that moment when conscience easily gave way to their higher power. Only after the smoke cleared and rose to the skies would they know pain for what they had to do with the bodies. Each man and woman of the village felt sickened by the sight of their work.

John found Harris curled up in a near-fetal position on the ground and brought him upright with one arm. "Tell me now, what would you do here?"

"Let me live, please," the Captain begged him, barely forming words. His quivering voice was less demanding than it had been before he met the Carolina battlefield. Many warriors gathered around the small group of prisoners found lying in the field. They had each become passive subjects of a Chief they could only hope would show them mercy.

"Tell me where you came from… in the north, man. You must confirm your nation, your place. This is the third time we have been pressed and shall be the last, as sure as I breathe. Your army cannot inhale even a scent of air in our home."

"I'm from that place Baltimore—the old city where Ostam rules," he quickly admitted.

"And it is there where your people cause others to come to the fire of our warriors? You bring men to our home—into early death. Why do you come here?"

"Yes, sir… Please spare me!" he said, able to speak clearly again. "I only follow orders. I only did my master's bidding to find a murderer."

"You failed to heed my word. There are no murderers here," John said as he looked across the field at the aftermath. "Your master… Who is he that assumes he has such a right to enter another nation?"

"Ostam, sir," Harris said, being respectful for the first time in his life toward anyone other than Ostam.

Jeremiah heard the brief but powerful explosion of sound from the area of old Asheville and knew what that meant. He felt trickles of water starting from his eyes. He stopped the line of children, quietly asking them to rest close together and telling them they must cover their ears. He was afraid screams would replace the sharp noise and fill the air with the awful sounds of human beings in agony. He asked the children to pray silently for safety.

He thought of Katherine, of John—and the rest of the family, his friends, the free nation. I caused this and was not with them, he thought as he swallowed hard against the guilt. He buried his head in his rough, calloused hands to hide his emotions from the children as best he could. I'm in a fix, not where I should be, and where I must be. I pray, dear Lord; let them be safe from that terrible army who will not know peace.

The distance was too great. He could not see the outcome, the result of another interlude of extreme violence, and he knew he had to wait. The children needed him. He was the only road they had to life and the man sworn to guide them there.

"I know his name, fool," John said. "Why does Ostam use death as his most beloved tool, his first and last resort? Who is he?"

Harris was speechless and worried now that he would be killed. He lowered his head and waited for the blow or shot—whatever form his execution would take. He could not run away. He could do nothing.

"You choose not to tell me what drives you people to come here. You cannot plot to kill us when we have done no harm to you or to your master without reason. Even the most vicious animals have reason to kill."

Harris raised his eyes slightly to look at the man who had him. "I do not know, sir. Have mercy on me, please. I beg you to let me live."

"You will live. We do not kill for thrill or glory—or nothing—as you do," John said. His face was contemplative as he waited; to Harris, the time seemed much longer. Am I to be shot at any moment? He lies. He will do what I would do. He is the killer in the mountains. He happens to have the guns now. John felt the urging from somewhere deep. What began months ago, as the smallest electrical current in his mind, had become a broad current of demand.

Other men and women—and surely children—were suffering in Baltimore. If it were not his divine mission, would there be anyone to take up the innocents' cause and deliver them? He closed his eyes and wrestled the pain away from between them. He stooped to within inches of Harris's face. "You help me stop Ostam. I will free the people held captive in your city. By doing that, we'll also finally stop these invasions, for we must be left to our own and not be in constant war over nothing."

He had nearly forty northern survivors gathered along with Harris and marched them into Asheville. The shell of an old warehouse would serve as the accumulation area where the strangers could be held, fed, and questioned. John put guards on them to ensure they posed no threat to the village.

"I will get you food," he said to the crowd of men, most of whom appeared exhausted. They all seemed frightened by the sight of these warriors, a foe unlike any they had ever seen or encountered before. "Do not try to harm our people here, and no harm shall come to you."

Chapter 20

Harris Meets Hungry Wolves

Harris could not accept the state he found himself in. He thought of escape and returning to Ostam to tell him of the trap—by thousands of armed men and how he bravely fought but had to retreat after losing all his men. He practiced the lie. Bullets ripping past me, but I fought back and killed many, he thought to report the lie. At last, I saw there were so many I had no choice but to make sure you know, master! He thought as he had in the past and was ready to return to his privilege.

Quiet settled in the valley once more. Jeremiah heard it and gathered his breath to take the children on to their mountain home. He began walking without saying a word as Matthew helped him urge the nine to follow him. The slopes appeared larger as they made their way toward them, alone. The three miles he covered was a peaceful trek, unmolested by man or beast. No one came toward them, nor were they lying in wait ahead.

The air was clean. The sun was gentle. Their path seemed perfect, as he could have hoped every prayer was answered for such relief. He sensed a special, though unseen, presence over all their precious heads and knew they were being protected by a power no mortal man can truly know or imagine. He was compelled to walk on, and each child followed him as surely and steadily as he. He did not stop. There was neither need nor time to rest.

No one was at the road entry of the old trail he had used so many times to begin the climb of the first mountain. They were close. Each child still stepped lively and seemed joyous. They were enjoying the work of foot travel with him as the mountains loomed ahead.

They came to the stream in the valley between the second and third spine of higher earth and new growth trees. They stopped for a minute to use the clean water to wash away the dust and dirt collected on their exposed skin while they walked so far. Home was close—as close as one more climb where they would meet the village. They would see Katherine, and Mathew's mother, Mary, would be there to hold her son once again. There promised to be the warmest acceptance by good American people of the Nation that worked and lived well, laughed, and thrived with each other deep in the rich, beautiful mountains of Carolina, safely welcomed in their portion of the great state, the new great nation.

Jeremiah could clearly see it all before them. He smiled widely as he watched the children splash and play in the stream. He heard them laugh for the first time since he met them in Baltimore.

Close now, children of an old state. You're going home and will never be forced to chain your hearts to another man of a different kind— the black heart of greed, murder, and slavery. Your freedom was promised from the first day when our brother Little Wolf spied those who would keep it for themselves. Now you're close. Laugh. Breathe. Feel. Be!

Jeremiah felt the ease of beautiful peace. He knew to be certain of John's outcome even though he didn't see it. He felt delivery through every muscle and across every stretch of skin, deep in his eyes and from within. He listened to the spirit and knew all was well. He would see Katherine soon. He would see John and the rest soon. He would embrace good old Jack.

"I see them coming!" she said excitedly. "It's Jeremiah! Come see him!" one of the women announced to those close to her.

"He's bringing little ones! Mary, Mary—is it your son?" Katherine said.

"Yes! Mathew!" Mary shouted as she ran to him and embraced him. "And you brought all of these precious children with you!"

Katherine embraced Jeremiah. "It is good that you're home!"

"I have dreamed of this moment, and it is everything I hoped for, dearest," he said as he once again felt her love and warmth. His dog, Jack, jumped up constantly as he cried with joy.

"Please bring them to the lodge where we will tend to them," Katherine said. "Mary, Sara, let us prepare food and a good place for them to rest!"

Jeremiah looked at Katherine and the women of the village. "Tell me about John and our warriors. Do you have news?"

"He is on the way, Jeremiah, and will be with us soon. The invader has been stopped again, and God was with us, as surely as He is restoring the earth before our eyes!"

"Let us give thanks then. The greatest Chief of all has delivered us home, and we must thank and honor Him."

John suddenly stepped into the open lodge and answered from the sunlight striking the opening, creating a blinding background to his figure.

"Jeremiah! It's good to see you, my friend!" he said. "Welcome home, warrior. You've done well."

"It is good to be home, John!"

"The children you brought here shall be ours now."

"I'll take care of them, John," Sara spoke first. "Please, let me. They are where I was not so long ago," she said, tears glistening on her cheeks.

"We all will help you, Sara. Thank you. Stars Light is happy and proud of you," John said. He turned back toward Jeremiah. "He was with us in the valley,

Jeremiah. I felt him give me the words. I followed him, as he was our guide. I know he led us to victory—God gave us the strength."

The celebration went well into the night with song, dance, and plenty of food and clean, pure water. John had some food prepared to take back to Asheville for the prisoners and the few guards. He didn't want to keep any of them long and would return the next day to set them free again, but without their guns. Those who desired could have freedom and join the work of the village. Those who wanted to leave could do so and travel to any place they desired. He would not stop them or interfere. The plan was set, and the elders agreed.

The strings played the happy sounds of music from their ancestors' time as many of the villagers danced to the rhythms, part Irish in nature, part Cherokee in delivery. A wave of laughter filled the lodge as glasses were raised, and the people expressed their joy through smiles and laughter. It was a very human celebration under twinkling skies of love and dignity, perfection and purity.

John lay down for some much-needed sleep. The village settled in and kept the children warm in Sara's cabin. Mary and Matthew stayed up for a while to consider their great fortune—and their great loss. Father and brother had been taken from them by an evil that still lived. They mourned them. "Never again," she said. "Never again, please, Lord," she prayed with her son.

Near Asheville, Harris thought he had a chance. He didn't know that if any of them moved, the guards would let them, as was the word of Chief John. John said he would not have any of Harris's men killed unless they tried to harm their hosts. As the warehouse became dark, he watched the guards as they casually moved around the broken walls. There weren't that many of them. All he had to do was avoid being a clear target while he ran to create a long distance between himself and these unders. There were plenty of openings to choose from where he could slip out and run for his life back toward Baltimore. His truck and extra fuel were waiting where he left them, though well outside Asheville, he figured. All he had to do was make it out of this place and cover the distance.

He waited until he didn't see a guard nearby and began moving slowly, quietly across the backs of his men who were lying in clusters, sleeping. He moved a little and stopped, waiting to know whether he was spotted. Nothing. He slipped toward the vertical crack in one of the building's corners where joists separated, forcing bent, weathered, and torn tin wall sections apart and revealing an opening just large enough for a man to use as an escape. He was close. Nothing. He slithered through the crack like a snake.

He waited outside for any sign of a guard to make sure it was still and safe. Nothing. He moved his legs and slowly pushed his body along the ground for yards, showing no profile against the starry sky and moonlit horizon. He quickly made it to the next city block and hid behind the wall of another old, partially destroyed building. He waited for any sign. Nothing. There were no indications his escape had been discovered. It was time to run further.

He ran as fast as he could move his legs. Across blocks of concrete streets and asphalt-covered roadways, he ran non-stop until he reached the outer limits of the city. There, the building foundations gave way to open fields. He stopped, doubled over, and sucked in as many breaths as his lungs could take, as rapidly as they allowed. His legs were wobbly as he gulped the sweet air that hovered in Asheville that night.

Harris looked out across an old field that lay in front of him, in the direction he ran. Perhaps it had once been inhabited by fine, beautiful horses. Maybe it was merely kept as an extravagant yard for the owners of the mansion set well back from the rest of the world. The property appeared to be separated by prestige in Asheville anyway. Now it was overgrown and rougher looking than when the privileged had paid to have it groomed and maintained—a wasted space for a few.

The mansion he could see in the distance was but a shell of its former self—only piles of rubble and rotting wood pieces jutting upward, made shorter by the harsh environment each passing year. Beyond the field and the homestead, the landscape rose and gradually sloped toward foothills leading to a larger range of mountains beyond his sight. He thought he was making his escape toward his army's demarcation point at the intersection that had been built on the flat. That was where he had them all dismount to attack and take the old city.

The persistent stench of putrid air punctured through a wide area. It was the escape of gases from his dead soldiers. He might have realized that had he thought of them. His only thoughts were centered on getting as far away from that strange Chief John and his superior army. It seemed to Harris that there must have been thousands of them. The southern unders laid a trap for him and dismantled his army piece by piece, as body by body fell flat to earth. In fact, less than three hundred souls had stopped him. Three hundred souls were willing to risk their lives for the sole purpose of stopping an invader.

Staying as low as he could while still quick-stepping, he crossed the field and began to handle the upward slope. The space between trees was sparse to begin with but started to close smaller and smaller with every fifty feet he made it up the incline. The trees were thick at the top and beyond, as far as he could see in the night, as he peered at what lay ahead from the summit of the first hill.

Though the area seemed unfamiliar to him, he followed his fear rather than his fading logic. He told himself he was traveling in the right direction in the few seconds of rational wonder that attempted to overstep his constant nightmare of the army that had just defeated him. He kept pushing deeper and deeper until the forest on high surrounded him and eliminated any skyline or horizon that could have aided his navigation.

He stumbled over ground roots that tripped him. He was unable to stop his fall and struck his face on the hard ground. Blood oozed from his broken nose; the pain caused his eyes to swell and water, taking his sight for a few critical minutes. He stopped to sit until his focus returned, using his shirt to wipe away the tears and blood. He figured he was far enough away and protected from his captors anyway. He thought that he could take some time to rest. He found a comfortable area to lie down.

He heard the first howl—a loud, long howl of one wolf—and then slowly another answered until he heard several sing out their natural calls. Fear piled on top of fear, causing him to shake; the convulsions within his body seemed to make every twig and rock announce his location to the wolf pack. Hearing himself brought on more fear.

New growth pines are not easy to climb as there are no branches to use and their thin straight trunks are difficult to grip very high up until one's arms can no longer support the weight of a human body for more than a few feet. Then one cannot hang on the vertical trunk for very long —before all the strength in his arms and legs is entirely depleted and he plummets back to the ground. The howls grew closer and sounded more excited. He knew they had found their kill, and it was to be him. Then the origins of the rough wolf music were nearer to him. Within a few agonizing but brief minutes, he could tell the animals had found the same ridge he occupied.

It was as if the pure spirit of Little Wolf, who gave his earthly life for his tribe, was present. His was the spirit force moving to defend his people once more against an enemy; a new time in this place for the deliverance of his nation. Now that same spirit has mapped the location of an enemy for the alpha wolf.

Part of Little Wolf's spirit returned in the form he knew and admired for the free spirit within the fur and behind the long teeth. It could have been some other power from a realm Harris did not believe existed that brought them. It could have been simply and solely hunger that fueled the instinct of ferocious animals to find him. Harris would never know.

Little Wolf would not have smiled over the impending death of another human being, but he understood the wolf. Should his spirit be able to speak, he might even save him, but he heard no plea and thus would do nothing but allow the wolf to have his meat. He was present for the time—in the place close to where he felt the viper's stinging strikes—and watched the pack encircle their prey and slowly close the distance between them and him.

Harris saw the first set of fiery eyes peering from between useless sticks that reached toward the darkness above. Through the narrowest of openings, he saw another set of cold, lighted eyes, then another slightly over from the first two. A slight, practically indiscernible touch of starlight reflected off teeth from every angle as he desperately searched for an escape. He was surrounded. He had nowhere to run. He would have to fight them to live—to have the slightest chance of survival.

He had no army in front of him, no great hall to shield him, no underlings to sacrifice for him. He was alone. The first wolf ran at him as he tried to use one of the thin trees to hide behind, but a second hungry predator sank his fangs into his back. Quickly, the largest wolf jumped to his unprotected neck and tore into it as if it were paper. He felt the sharp sting; the pain was unlike anything he had experienced as he fell, unable to move. He knew he was losing consciousness. The faint blackness behind his eyes pulled him down into a weak, shaking mass, able to feel his body being eaten. The wolves tore into more of his flesh, ripping deeper and deeper into his body; his last hope for relief was a quick death, so far an elusive desire. Soon it would be over for him, and the meat would at least serve some good for the land. Feeding other mammals would be his life's final and only good offering.

His screams went unheard by anyone as he lost small portions of his stomach fat and sides that were torn off in chunks and quickly chewed up. Only the black and gray wolves heard his screams and then the whimpers just before death while they devoured more of his soft, juicy flesh—to them, a feast for each adult in the pack and every cub waiting in the den. Almost every one of his bones was broken into pieces, morsels. Only a portion of his torso along with a skull was left for other scavengers in the light of the morning. The place Harris last set out to conquer was marked. One Captain of Baal left a wide stain of blood residue, small slices of bone, and tissue to mark his invasion.

The guards finally brought him a cup of water. James had been tied up in the room long enough for Lee's body to begin to decompose. Deep breaths caused him to gag. He could go nowhere and assumed he would receive the same fate as Lee. Through his clouded mind, he heard a cluster of hard steps coming toward the room.

Suddenly, a detail of six soldiers burst through the door. Two of them pulled the stiff body out while the four others turned their attention to James. Lee's body was on its way to the pigs. James was cut loose and promptly slapped across his already swollen face. They dragged him out too.

His first thoughts after shaking off the cloud that had covered his mind were of Julie. He hadn't found her. He hadn't heard her sweet, reassuring voice in days and had no idea what they had done to her.

Of everything he was, of everything that was important in his life—that meant life—Julie was and is the most important, his greatest loss because of his abduction. In the world as it had become, even in Indianapolis, the woman Julie was his hope. He felt their hands grip his arms to hold him fast. The pressure was like steel vices squeezing the flesh against bone to ensure he could not escape.

They took him to face Ostam. The leader, who preferred to be called Great Leader, was already seated in the plush oversized symbol of authority of his highest rank. On either side of him sat the mostly new court in smaller chairs. There had been some openings lately that now included a few in the bureaucracy. The new court began their tenure more subdued than Sands, Gack, and even Rachel had been.

The old court had been with Ostam from the beginning and helped him establish the laws that forbade firearms, limited births, and set in motion the status and class of every person in Baltimore—pushed on the populace as necessary for the sake of the children, the share of food, and their equal use of allowed resources still available. It was their good cause; their rewards had been exactly, and paradoxically, an unequal share of goods and services. They each had convinced themselves it was only right for them to have much more than the rest.

"Bring him in," Ostam said softly; his commands were less confident and issued in a quieter tone. He had yet to hear good news from Harris and feared the worst.

James was brought before him and made to stand. Two of the soldiers still held him as he painfully stood to face his penalty, his torment. His jaw hung toward his chest. He chose to avoid looking at anyone in the hall.

"Tell me why you left the room we gave you," the Great Leader asked. "We provided you with food, a job, and dry, warm shelter for your sleep… we told you to stay there, and yet you defied our orders. Why?"

James didn't answer. The guards on both sides of him pushed hard against his sides to make him speak. "I wanted to find my friend Lee and…," he said and stopped, thinking that if he mentioned he was looking for Julie too, he would be putting her in jeopardy.

"That Lee—he defied us the whole time he's been here, under," Ostam said, disgust dripping from his voice. "We gave him everything, yet he would not work with us."

James said nothing.

"What should we do with you then? Do you intend to teach our people in exchange for your comfort here?"

James knew it was his last chance to comply. Unable to form words that could be heard, he nodded. Agreeing to do so was his only chance to see Julie again. Resigning himself to serve this master and accept his fate as a loyal, though unhappy, government worker was the only way. He knew that he was, in fact, a slave.

He would most likely come to believe he was satisfied, at least able to tell himself that much. He felt their grip tighten as the soldiers returned him, on Ostam's gesture, back to his room where the minor wounds would heal over time without any care provided by the state. He was an under— a high under—but an under nonetheless.

Chapter 21

"May I speak to you, John?" Mary asked the Chief.

"Yes, of course, Mary. How's your son Matthew? Is he going to be happy here?" he asked hopefully.

"Oh yes, he's fine and very happy. He already says he wants to learn carpentry from Tom Whittle and Big Bear." She smiled with pride.

"It is a new way for him—just as it is for you, Mary. How is everything going for you?" he asked.

"Life here is wonderful, John… and I thank you with all my heart for helping me—and the warrior Jeremiah who bravely went to find my son. I have never experienced so much love as I have here with these people," she said, weeping.

He waited for her to speak more while embracing her as a close friend.

"This nation, this way… is why I wanted to speak to you."

"Yes?" he asked to prompt her.

"Chief… there are many people in Baltimore who are filled with love and faith yet suffer horribly in ways I can't begin to describe well enough—but we are only two of them you took into your heart." She glanced down, unsure what she was asking of him. "I don't know how to help the rest, and yet I am compelled to try," she said as she began to cry.

"Are there not people who would rise up against tyranny?" he asked. The concept was as foreign to him as Harris and the soldiers who came to the valley. How can people not change their nation? Why would they settle for such a life? Man was born to be free and of goodwill. That pierces through any pretense of structure like the one they have in Baal. Why has there not been a revolution, even a peaceful one? No, there can be no peace with those who enslave for greed. Fear—fear of dying, fear of slaughter, and fear of being fed to the pigs—is more powerful than the misery of not being free. It's a shame, an awful place for anyone to exist, he thought.

He knew that not all men were like him, though. Some are meek and subservient, taking each day of life as just one more day of serving another to live enough to breathe, if not much more. Some find a measure of contentment by serving even the vilest captain. John's head sank to his chest. It was a heavy burden.

Though he had thoughts in the deep layers of his mind of going to Baal to stop any further attacks, he knew from history that such efforts rarely work with such tribes. It had to be done with power. Whether it was solely greed that drove some to kill other human beings or fear or the purest form of envy, he didn't know. How could he know why so much violence had been and is still heaped upon others? How could he hope to stop what had led the peoples in this place Baal made for a great number of survivors? The place they were now couldn't be understood except through the sorry history of all mankind.

Now Harris was gone. Instead of helping free people, the man decided to leave and return to the center of death. John knew he might miss the chance to be free. Years of submersion in such a way do not prompt one to step out into another, different world. The most informed source of intelligence in Baal did what John expected—reverting to what he knew. The man has no desire for freedom. He is lost, John thought.

"Mary, Mary… your heart is right and good. You cry for people you know who are held captive—who are used by that horror that is the invaders' nation. Are we to take up the cause for them? I will bring it to the elders and the people of the village." The Chief was unsure whether the people in Baltimore would want a different way.

"I don't know what is right. I don't know if our people should die for them. I'm sorry to worry you, Chief. I pray for another way, if only there were another way," she said as she uncomfortably turned her face away from him.

He understood her contradiction and the mixed emotions swirling inside her as she thought about so many far away in the iron grip of a powerful enemy. He felt the same. The idea of any more losses to the nation terrified him. The truth that he knew of suffering and could choose to do nothing made him heartsick.

"I must take the issue to our elders, Mary. They are people of heart and spirit and need to hear."

She slowly raised her head and quietly said, "If we go, Matthew and I must go too."

"I know you would," he said. He gazed out at the vast sky above their mountain and thought of how it covered all—the people he knew and the people he didn't know. Everyone feels its warmth and sees its beauty—feels its hope and space, the many delights it provides for the eyes, and the many warnings it generously supplies too. If everyone could see the vast above through simple eyes, more would come to understand how we share a common start. We are all the same, and yet man's weaknesses change some as they live years beyond innocent youth. I changed too. We all change. If I were able to reach the good spirit inside those who kill, would they embrace the part of them that is good?

It is not within many to discard their greed though. Their hearts have shriveled to a small speck with no beauty. Their spirits are ugly remnants of what once was given to them freely, and death fuels what is left of them—little nuggets of hate for hate's sake. Yes, we will discuss going to Baal. We will bring our free hearts to the cause. Our lives are best spent for others, after all, as it is written in better words than I possess in thought.

Each day that passed meant more torture up north—one place he knew of where liberty had become a foreign, unused word. He knew he had to move quickly because of that, and he knew the elders were of the same mind and would agree. He knew the village warriors would take on the cause as gladly as they had taken on Raymond, Dobey, Morford, and Harris—that regardless of the numbers and danger, they would take on the cause. His shoulders felt heavy. He carried the weight through the pain it pressed into his heart.

The lodge was somber that night as John brought the issue to them. They knew he would and, before he spoke, knew exactly what their only moral answer could be. Yes, of course, the horror must be stopped by the hands of the American nation. Yes, of course, they would go and do all they could to free people.

Troubles come for responsible people who believe in more than their own pleasure—a constant truth. When evil works its worst, it must be stopped and quashed until it dares not even raise its ugly hand to request a respite because the knives of good must slash against it. It will never stop. The duty that guides men of good will and pure heart, living their intentions to defend the defenseless, never stops if all that is true. Hurry! Each day could mean death to another little one!

"John, there are strangers approaching!"

"Let us go meet them," he said.

John and Jeremiah took the trail out of the village and saw a small group of men, women, and children walking toward the nation as if they knew the way.

"Hello to you. We are of the nation, and you have entered our mountain. Why do you come?"

The man leading the small entourage said, "We heard of a place, a place where there is work and food, sir."

"Yes…" he said. He had just begun to answer when his attention was diverted by several sources of noise and children. Another small group came toward them, and then another emerged through the pines, and another, all using different trails to make their way toward the summit.

Jeremiah gently touched the trigger guard of his .44, just in case he would have to use it. "Please stop here," he said, pointing toward the spot of earth just in front of him. He stared at the pitiful sights advancing toward where he and John stood to stop them.

They had the unmistakable look of hunger. Made thin by time and the lack of food—except for the children, who appeared better fed—the adults did as they were asked. The faces of every stranger were turned down in humility as though they were begging for mercy. He noticed their clothing was not so much clothing as fixed tatters, barely covering most of their bodies. He saw their possessions included some old worn blankets, a few old packs, half-empty, and a number of rusty and aged rifles slung over some of their shoulders. These people have traveled a long way to get here, he thought.

"We'll feed you and the children. Please follow us a little further," John said.

The few armed men in front unslung their rifles and began to surrender them to Jeremiah. John noticed the gesture and said they could keep their rifles—keep them hanging across their backs. He saw no threat on their faces and felt no threat from their hearts. "Come this way," he said.

The strangers came into the village—a place unlike any they had ever visited before. Maybe in old movies they watched as children and dreamed of as a scene in an adventure, the village was a sight of welcome and warmth, everything they had hoped for in their years of struggle. It was a return to a simpler time, a happier time, a place of friendliness, a place where one had no fear of what another would do to steal.

"My dreams... call them an urging of some kind..." one of the men said aloud. "I was brought here from Texas by something I can't see. I felt it," he said and cried. "Thank you. Thank you." They followed John and Jeremiah into the lodge. Jack quietly got up and moved outside.

"Take your own space to rest. You're welcome here," Jeremiah said as he began handing out cups of water to them all. Katherine and Sara brought them food, and others followed with one plate after another.

"Tell me, traveler, what caused you to come to us?" Jeremiah asked the man seated next to him.

"We heard of your house of peace and of your fights against invaders. Those invaders have gone out and killed many, and everywhere they go, they take what little was left, you know, after the war... there are still many good people alive out there," he said and stopped. "Many of us are mighty tired of wondering if they'll come for us next."

"Where do you hail from?"

"Texas, sir," he said with a proud grin. "We heard they came to Houston and murdered people for a little food and to take everything they could for themselves. Most of us are from what was Dallas," he said. Jeremiah noticed he seemed excited to tell more. The man began laughing. "Yeah, we found one of them running away from y'all! He told us all about it. Said his name was Dobey... he was on his way to California—and we figured he could have it," he said and laughed. "We let him go about his way but took his guns." He laughed. "He had some fine pieces."

"So that's where you heard about these mountains?"

"Yeah, and what he said was true, isn't it? You all fought them off and turned them back to the north?"

"Yes, we did. Had to, you understand. Some people just can't leave others alone."

"Yeah, they came into Houston… murdered men, women, and children there," he looked down, clenched his teeth, and furrowed his brow, anger and hate clearly etched across his face Jeremiah could see. "Course Houston… poor Houston was lost long ago. I won't say any more about that but the ones left there didn't deserve to die like they did, in the streets—hunted like a pack of rabid animals," the man was unable to clearly finish his words because he was choking up and unable to speak past the torment of deep heartache for all of them.

"You're right, traveler. No one deserves that except those who do it."

"And you turned them into ground pudding up here! I want to help y'all do that!" The life in his face returned.

"Well, we only do what we have to do. They came here to hurt our people. We stopped them, that's all, and we had people die because of it. It's our right to defend ourselves," Jeremiah said, looking away from the stranger who talked as if he wanted violence. He wanted to talk to someone else about what brought so many to the mountains at one time. He thought about it and told the man that they are a peaceful village and do not want war or killing. "I hate killing. We all hate killing. If that is why you're here, you should leave us." He locked eyes with the traveler.

"I only thought… I mean, I just want to…"

"Not in our nation, sir. That is not why we live."

"Please give me a chance. I lost a sister in Houston, that's who I think about all the time… no reason for them to do to her what they did. I wished I'd been there," he said, his voice quivering.

Jeremiah reached toward the man's back, touched the taut, leathery surface through his worn-out shirt to accept him. "I'm sorry. Eat, drink, and rest, traveler. You're welcome here and your cause is just," he said. "Just know the nation didn't start this war. It's not in us. We'll die to stop it."

Jack returned to Jeremiah for his dinner. He moped around his master's seat until the man understood what he was asking. Jeremiah fixed the dog a plate and smiled as he watched his old friend lap down morsels, barely chewing the pieces of meat from his dish.

"We must move on, Baal. I see no other course for our nation. We've grown stronger and our best chance to end what has become constant wars is to dig the root up and throw it into the river, drown it for our sake and for the sake of the people who asked for none of this," John said to the elders gathered deep in the night at the lodge. The nation was asleep and taking comfort in dreams of peace and the hope they had for a bright tomorrow. The new citizens took their places along the edges of the forest, breathed the clean air of the mountains while others were inside many of the cabins, using the larger front rooms to stretch out without fear.

"I know we must," Jeremiah said. He was asked to join them after his unselfish work. He turned his head down. The moment was but another serious moment that broke into the peaceful day work the nation loved—this one though was to discuss and decide on war. It was a heady task, the darkest subject, which no single person in the leadership relished or wanted. The elders—men and women who built the village on the place left for them by those who came before—were close to John and leaned closer toward the man who saw Stars Light die that horrible day when the new burden was forced on them all.

"There may be many who will not return," John said. "I don't know the horizon we'll see after… it's dark and covered in my mind, ladies and gentlemen. Vision has failed me on this… while I know well the answer for the nation; I don't know the answer for me. It is you who must decide, and we must be in one accord."

"What other measure can we take?" Katherine said, her hand gently resting in the folds of Jeremiah's calloused hands he held close to her.

"If we leave them, they will take more lives there and will come here again. I believe there's no doubt that would mean miserable war again in our whole future. Despots have never stopped, never retreated to a better place, you know. As long as he lives and has power, he will use that power against people," Jeremiah said, forming his words thoughtfully, carefully. "Is that not true? Tell me, please. Has it not always been the warped pleasure these men get out of causing the same pain that destroys them?"

John looked up. "It has, Jeremiah—many have done their worst until they themselves die for it—after killing so many," he said. "That's why we are a new nation after all and why we must proceed… it is for us, a sacred duty."

"I believe we have this chance today," one of the elders said after deliberating silently until this moment. "Our ancestors were at times on it —but always late it seems. Sometimes, they did nothing. In both cases, more people suffered than should have."

"Are we all in agreement?" John said, looking past the crowd toward the night sky he saw outside. He knew the young warriors would not hesitate. Given a choice, and being free to volunteer, none would decline the fight for liberty. It wasn't in them to avoid the fight, and he would be putting them at risk exactly because of their idealism, a code shared throughout the village.

"When shall we go?" a voice asked firmly.

"We shall go as soon as we're prepared," John said. He turned away from the gaze into the night. "Please bring your hands together and vow with me that this is the decision of the elders."

There was no dissenter.

As the solemn group placed their hands together, Jeremiah watched outside of his own as the stars seemed to dance, several streaked across the blackness, and he knew that each could be a sign from the world he has yet to join. A single tear erupted from one of his eyes and followed a track down his cheek and neck. He thought of those who were no longer on earth. He felt the beats of his parents' hearts as they were and saw their eyes joining them again for the greatest work that lay ahead.

Ostam was rambling around the hall, large enough for echoes to raise the specter of losing everything. He couldn't stand still, could barely think; each idea that came to him was cut off by his mind too soon to comprehend. His pace began as a slow walk while he tried to sort it out but soon became frenetic. Every sound that pierced the quiet caused his head to turn convulsively toward its source. Nightfall brought the city rain, and though the water was still cold, the ground was warmer. Fog slowly rose from the concrete and steel like nature's desperate last showing as it witnessed yet another war.

Chapter 22

To Baltimore Again

John gathered the warriors to move on Baal. The nation found Harris's vehicles easy enough to use and employed them to shorten the journey north. The army was a quiet, contemplative group of men and women putting aside their comforts to stop the source of their horrors. Jeremiah once again left the village and Katherine to return to Baltimore and be with his brothers and sisters. Pushing away thoughts of whom they might lose as if he could foresee tragedy, he watched John moving forward with the resoluteness of stone. It is easy to pray; it is harder to do the work. He bowed his head anyway as the truck he was in jumped and jerked through potholes and missing concrete on the old interstate.

The mountain people's army rode the push of nature swirling toward the north. Mary forced her mind to put aside her driven hate in order to coolly lead them to the place where being a slave took from every minute, every hour of life. She witnessed their stifled speech and thoughts, their constant misery in Baal, and their deaths, which were so routine, so very meaningless.

For many, it was as natural to simply stop being and die inside while breathing Baal's rancid air just so their bodies could have another morning. In Ostam's city, such was the state that most were in the prison of slavery and were mere chattel to be exchanged for anything the higher class, the court, or Ostam desired more than anything freely given by nature herself. Mary touched the backs of every warrior while crying. She gave them comfort for their journey to war, for some, what was to be their last journey on earth. It was the right thing to do.

The wave grew into a powerful, constant wind that included Little Wolf, Stars Light, Paul, Victor, and the many faces of the fallen taking their place among the low clouds above the force. Unseen, silent sentries accompanied them in front and on the sides of columns of men and women rolling toward Baal, the fallen keeping vigilance against harm to the warriors. John sensed their presence nearby.

Their numbers had swollen overnight with people who came from Texas, Alabama, South Carolina, Tennessee, and Virginia. The one hundred new citizens who came to the free nation humbly asked for admittance. They had now joined the nation in war against an enemy they recognized from the carnage he left behind. Streams of a few good people guided by hope came into the village during the happy day after Harris was met and destroyed. The nation grew in strength and resolve that day.

No storms, no enemy, no hunger slowed them. The great wind of reckoning was moving toward Ostam and his. Soon, dear providence, soon… a change will come to the people of Baltimore not because many in their number deserve it but because they are to be freely given the chance to deserve it. Then, it must be their moral free will that guides them in knowledge of what is good and right, and that must be allowed to flourish at any cost; they shall make the choice for themselves and live in peace.

The American village will be protected by destroying the one who sets violence upon it—who is compelled to kill them. The new village of the north must take its own course and enjoy its own use of freedom, if they will, if they can guard against the same mindset of evil and misuse of government utility of those who came before them. That was before the darkest days of Ostam when it was allowed to build and swallow more human beings under the guise of caring so much that freedom had to be slowly but surely consumed—the banquet of elites who cared far more about their own pleasures than the people who put them into power.

Sometime after daylight, the warriors set foot and left the array of vehicles they had used to get as close as the fuel allowed them. Most were stopped at the same time somewhere just south, near old Washington D.C., where men and women had failed in the past. The old leaders lost their world, coldly witnessing the total collapse of a strangled, convoluted economic system, and finally the violent death of millions of people, before feeling its slow work on their own until even these elites knew nothing more. The result of their hard hearts, lies, deceit, hate, and unquenchable greed could portend no more certain results.

Jeremiah saw the remnants of old D.C. and thought how very good it was to be marching through her heart to face the product of her intercourse with simple, single-minded human pigs who talked and talked, and begged and begged, but stole all they could. The leaders of the time fooled them, pretending to be the only true friends of the people, when it was more for themselves they wanted—and they took everything.

He saw the monuments and reflected on how grand the idea was behind them—how truly good the ideals posited were at their base. He knew that every ideal left for tourists to see was easily washed out. The ideals had been quashed long ago. The words were nothing more than etchings. Something else took their place because of the nature of man—and there were those who loved power more than any ideal. That was as it has always been and doesn't change with time—the unrestrained aggressors have always taken. Freedom in those last days had indeed become only a seldom-used word and an even less thought-about concept.

The nation marched on toward Baltimore. The city loomed before them. Soon, the warriors saw the skyline and outline of buildings jutting up like old monoliths of power, prestige, and money that once was. The first to enter the ghetto of the unders included Jeremiah, Katherine, John, and several village warriors. The stench filled the air around them as curious people of the ghetto came to see them. Who are the people who are with us now and armed? It frightened most of them, fearing that an army had come to kill them all.

The bravest woman of the under village stepped out of the gathering crowd of entrails eaters to face Jeremiah. The unders near her said that she was once a mother. She knew that she was still a mother, though her son David had withered to a scant leathery resemblance of a human being who once lived. He was now nothing more than a nearly skeletal form buried deep in a hole underground. Jeremiah knew that she was one who had learned much. He saw her mournful eyes and understood them. She had lost everything and was still sick with grief, beyond angry, broken away from fear—a clean break, an irreversible want for revenge, and a craving for justice even in her weak form.

"Who are you?" she asked him.

"We are visitors here, ma'am. The people from this city have been attacking us for months, and we're here to stop them."

"I don't understand that answer. Are you not Ostam's army?"

"No. We must find him, though."

"What do you want with him?" she asked hopefully.

"We are here to stop him."

The ghetto, being a low priority, had only one guard posted nearby from the army. He saw the massive numbers of invaders and ran back to the city to report to his superiors. "They've come here, Captain!" he screamed out, out of breath from the run, stopping the newest Captain in the officers' club with those few words. The Captain left the building and hurried to see for himself.

He ran toward a vantage point in the building where he could see the ghetto. On the way, he ordered the men he saw to stand and follow him. As he rounded one building, he saw an army in the distance and felt sick, losing the contents of his stomach to the cracked sidewalk below. He saw a strange, new, and dangerous army marching out of the ghetto and toward the center of the city. He ran back to tell Ostam that they were under assault from an overwhelming, unknown force.

"He will come to you, sir. Some here may join you. Would you let a woman help you?" the under woman asked.

Jeremiah looked into her eyes again. "Yes, ma'am… of course. Joining us is dangerous for you, though," he said.

"I do not care about that, sir."

He saw others slowly come toward them and turned toward John.

"These are the people I saw, John."

John took the woman's hand and told her she was welcome to help the nation.

"He will know about you soon," she said. "He'll try to kill all of you," she managed to say in a broken voice, her eyes welling with tears of worry for them.

"Let him know," he said. "Where do we find him, madam?"

"You will find him in the great hall in the center of the city, sir. That is where he rules this place. It is the large building with lights about two miles away."

"We must be on our way then. Please take your place after the last warrior steps through. We wish you no harm. You have lost much already and shall lose no more," John said knowingly.

Others came closer and stared at the strange-looking group of men and women who had arrived so suddenly. One voice cried out that he would gladly give them all the food he had—and others would help too. Many felt a surge of energy unlike anything they had experienced before, drawing them closer to the marching nation. They knew they were good and were there to deliver them.

Voices began to cry out with offers of anything they needed—they were happy to give these strangers, these helpers, anything and everything they had. Hope came in the form of leather-clad visitors who bravely shouldered rifles and marched as one. There was no doubt that Ostam was close to his last hour.

Ostam received the news and commanded the Captain to stop them at the ghetto. "Do whatever you have to do to stop them! Kill them all!"

"There are many, master," the Captain said, knowing his cause was futile.

"They've come here to kill us, Captain! You must stop them! Move! Now!" Ostam shouted.

The Captain didn't tell him that their numbers had already passed through the under village. He saw the wretched face of his leader and suspected he was about to run away. He knew they would be defeated and Ostam's empire was finished. He thought maybe he could begin the fight and then talk to the invaders to save himself. It was his only chance to survive this situation and forget Ostam. His orders meant nothing compared to what was coming their way. Too many of their number were miles away, killing and stealing.

As soon as the Captain disappeared down the hallway to follow his orders and march the small army to their deaths, Ostam gathered his suitcase of gold pieces and grabbed the arm of one of the slave girls to make his escape. He ran to the basement and its old parking garage. He had a fast car waiting with a full tank of gas. He knew the Captain and what was left of his army would fight to give him just enough time to make his getaway.

Jeremiah was the first to see the figure dodging in and out from behind a building that lay in their path to the hall. He readied his rifle and brought it up to his chest, prepared to fire. He did not stop the march, and the sights of his rifle were soon fixed on whoever it was. The unstoppable wind pushed through block after block until Ostam's Captain was found. He used an old-fashioned symbol of peace to save his life and held up a white flag.

Jeremiah saw the white cloth and took strong, sure steps toward the man. The Captain kept as low a profile as he could and was nearly bent over in half from fear as he waved the flag furiously over his head with one hand.

"Show your weapon!" Jeremiah called out with a force the Captain had never heard before, even from Ostam. "Now place it on the ground!"

He quickly did as he was told and began to feel safe. Jeremiah stepped toward him until he was face to face with one of their foes. The warrior knew that if the enemy wasn't weak, he wouldn't have one already surrendering. He appeared to be an officer or something, judging by the trinkets he wore on his shirt—a cheap sign Ostam awarded to those who were loyal and held some level of responsibility.

Jeremiah shouldered his rifle and replaced it with his .44. He held the pistol on his prisoner and walked him a few steps back to John. John wasted no time. Their mission was unfolding, and the time was now.

"Tell me about the army. How many are there, and where are they waiting?" John asked him.

"I am the Captain, sir. We are few—some are behind that building," he said, pointing to the bank building directly in front. "Others are over there, sir." He pointed toward the old insurance office complex. "The rest have taken flight."

"We will see," John said. "We'll have to hurry then," he said as he turned to catch Jeremiah's eyes. "Have them all lay down their arms, and we shall not harm them. You must do that now, Captain."

"Yes, sir!" He quickly turned toward the city to call out his order to the rest of Ostam's men who remained close.

"They must all come out," Jeremiah reminded him. The Captain complied.

After their unarmed prisoners were lined up with the warriors as they marched deeper into the city, John and Jeremiah saw the pig farm, a massive fenced area with heaps of filth and hundreds of animals moving around like a swarm waiting to be fed. That was in fact what they did while they bred.

John called for the Captain to come to him.

"Tell me, where is the hall, as it's called?"

"It's just ahead… a few blocks from here. Be wary of the guards still there, for they may still fight, sir. They're not like us."

Jeremiah knew he was telling the truth. He nodded to John.

The black luxury sedan raced out of the city using a northbound road, well away from the army that had taken his city. Ostam veered onto the old interstate and could see his chance. All he had to do was quickly spread the distance to be safe and free. He hadn't heard the shots yet and figured that meant the invaders had stopped to plan or something else an army does before battle. He didn't know nor did he care.

"I'll take half, Jeremiah, and move around the hall to the south. Will you take half and move to the north?"

"Yes, Chief John, of course!"

"We'll divide our forces and leave many to defend our line. That way, if we face unexpected strength, there'll be a reserve force ready to rush them."

"I understand. Godspeed, John. Please take good care and do the work that must be done."

"…And the same to you, Jeremiah," John said, the importance of the moment not lost on either man. "If I die, please tell the nation to carry on and not let our nation go the way of the past."

Within minutes, warriors were at every building, intersection, and walkway that encircled the city building. The hulks of vehicles, piles of concrete rubble, and the building itself were massive and covered large areas. Old statues erected decades ago to honor failed politicians, and remnants of shrub and tree stands were unused by any living growth and provided possible cover for the enemy.

Intermittent firing began as the warriors approached. Soldiers who were most loyal to Ostam began to nervously fire at them blindly, their shots scattering. They hit no one from the village. As the greatly outnumbered force tried to kill as many as they could, their eyes could not see the human targets clearly. One sniper stood behind a large window on the third floor and fired round after round at the warriors, missing every one of them. In return, several braves poured streams of lead toward him. The hail of bullets cut through his neck, releasing the head from the body as the dead torso and attached limbs fell with a thump onto the terrace and then to the ground below.

Jeremiah, having been to the place recently, knew much of the layout inside the building. He would lead his warriors into the center from the side door and take it for the nation. He had no doubts about whether the nation would prevail.

"Please stay here, Katherine. The reserve force John requested is coming up behind us. We need you and the others to be ready and come on signal. I'll send a runner when it's time."

"If that is what you want, Jeremiah, I will," she said.

"It's important, dearest, as we must keep a foundation to assure victory. Should we fail, it will be yours, and you must succeed, else our deaths will be in vain."

Another Ostam soldier lost control of his impulses and rushed toward the line of warriors, firing wildly. He managed to wound two village citizens before he was quickly cut down, becoming nothing more than a bloody heap of torn flesh and exposed bone. Katherine witnessed it and became sick to her stomach.

Inside the hall, the court and their entourages gathered in Ostam's seat of power. They nervously waited for the soldiers to repel the advancing invaders. There were no discussions now of another outrage to put on unders. There was no talking. They were quiet. There were no orders to be given to anyone nor any new laws to be enacted. They waited with fading hope that their lives would remain the same, for they had much to lose.

As the men and women of high status pondered what was happening around them—and outside what they thought was an impenetrable fortress, the engineer and others from Indianapolis made their way to an electrical utility room just off the parking deck in the basement. They were safe from the carnage. The solid steel door muffled the sounds of gunfire from inside and outside the building.

Julie knew that James was somewhere in the building. She wanted to find him and bring him to the place where she thought they were all protected. She looked at the few others and said she had to find James and would be back as soon as she found him. She slowly opened the door and peered outside for any sign of soldiers. She stepped out, surveyed the deck in a full circle to make certain it was clear, and then ran to the stairwell vestibule. Nearby, she heard rifle and pistol shots, but she kept running up the stairs. She knew he would not be on the first floor, as that was her floor. She ran up the second flight of stairs and slowly opened the door to the hall.

Each step brought her closer to either finding James or encountering Ostam's soldiers. After quickly passing several rooms without seeing James, she found a soldier lying dead inside, blocking the fourth door open, motionless. Beside him was his weapon—her one chance to defend herself. Jumping inside and quickly grasping the rifle, she turned to ensure she was not a target of another soldier. She checked the rifle for ammunition and inspected the bolt and receiver to make sure it was operable before leaving the dead body to venture further.

Ostam saw the road to old Frederick and turned onto the old interstate that would take him west. The woman he kidnapped was curled up next to her door in fear. He pushed the accelerator hard and nearly brought the sedan up on two wheels as he came to a curve.

John saw the entry he had used before and two or three figures in flashes positioned nearby behind the stone half-wall that shielded the lower entrance to the ground floor of the hall. He jumped out and ran toward the side of their cover to take them from the right on the horizontal plane inside the wall. His warriors trained their rifles at every point along the top edge to cover him.

He ran and didn't hear any firing from the wall. Making his way to the side of the vestibule, he saw that there were five soldiers cowering behind the concrete protection, their weapons hidden beside them. He called out to them, "Lay your weapons down! The nation has come, and you are our prisoners!"

The five complied, and four of them were led back to the reserves to guard. Jeremiah kept one to use as a guide inside the building. Their weapons were gathered up and handed over to other warriors to carry in the final assault. Jeremiah waved his warriors to come to him. He asked the prisoner to tell him quickly what was waiting inside.

"How many of you are inside?" Jeremiah asked, noticing a hint of hesitation on the prisoner's part. "Tell me quickly if you want to live!"

"There are seventy or so inside."

"Where are they?"

"They are mostly on the third floor, last time I knew. Some are scattered around other places."

"I want you to go with me and tell them to give up. You can tell them that the force in your city is very large, and if they want to live, they'll put their arms down. Got that?"

The prisoner nodded.

Jeremiah sent a runner to tell John he was making an entry. He firmly held the prisoner's arm and led forty warriors quickly through the door into the center of power. He led them into the center where a few people and one man decided everything for everyone else. He burst into the heart of greed and corruption where only a few prosper by taking freedom away from everyone they threatened with the gun. As he revisited the body of the demon, he felt its sickness, its tortured use of collectivism to enslave, to kill, to be—the proud, vain, faux superiors of others—who were convinced of their own superiority and so their own right to take and dole out what they saw fit.

The soldiers he found inside were weeping, scared, and quickly gave up the fight in groups until the warriors reached the large ornate double wooden doors.

He asked the prisoner who was inside the room.

"That's Ostam's hall," he said, his voice quivering and trailing off because of the fear of what he was revealing.

"He's in here?" Jeremiah asked as he pointed to the oversized entry.

"Yes. He would be inside."

Julie found James upstairs and heard the silence of the shooting. Not knowing what it meant, she proceeded to take him to the utility room. She saw the first warrior, who had a strange look—not like the soldiers—and fell to the floor, not knowing what he would do. There was nothing but a look in her direction. She looked up toward him and saw that others had suddenly appeared in the hallway.

"Push your weapon out, ma'am," the young warrior said. His voice was kind. He sounded different than the soldiers. She did as he asked and rose to her knees. James followed her and did the same.

"Who are you?" he asked and smiled.

"I'm Julie, and this is James. We're from Indianapolis and are prisoners here."

"You are prisoners no more, ma'am. Follow us, and we'll protect you."

"There are others, sir—hiding downstairs…"

Before she could say more, he told her that they would find them too and protect them all.

Jeremiah put a .44 round into the lock on the door, releasing it for entry. The court heard the shot and fell to the floor. Their servants and workers stood close to their masters, speechless, unable to move, frozen in indecisiveness. He ran into the center, and warriors peeled off each side behind him. The room was secure without a shot being fired. The battle was over and won. He sent a runner to John, who was advancing his warriors toward the grotesque concrete and steel monument of government gone insane.

"We do not want to take. We came to free," John began. "To take would destroy our truth, and we would become you," he said to the court. "Where is Ostam?"

One of the court members said he had taken flight and was no longer in Baltimore. Ostam had made his way to the outskirts of Frederick when he had to stop the sedan because the roadway was impassable due to vehicles and debris left years ago. The road was left as it was in the days of the great fires. He could go no further except by foot. He walked on, never to be seen or heard from again. He left his captive to fend for herself, but she was free.

Later, some thought he died on route from a heart attack or something similar, but no one knew with certainty what became of him. The unders were now people and had a chance for life. John made sure that they had food and water before taking his warriors home. He told them that they had to decide how to live. He told them that freedom works best when they return to the old book and the old commandments of God Himself.

"There's no need—hear me well—there's no need to complicate the matter of life on earth with laws and rules made by man, who always comes to be for himself. Be wary of anyone who would promise much in return for your loyalty. That word loyalty, used by the few, is another way of saying less freedom for you."

Within the next few months, in what was California, Ostam found people and what he thought was a weak leader and planned her elimination. He waited in a dark corner of the government building for his chance. To watch for the woman walking alone and take her with a long knife would give him a chance to promise life to the few hundred people and own Los Angeles.

Until the day of our Lord, there will be evil on earth. Only when His day comes will evil be no more.

The End

It is right as you know but we were and are still sadly, truly a body
of the weak,

In spirit, heart and life many thought to be counted high, ner' among
the meek,

Now you have rightly pressed man, father time; its past late for truth
to seek.

We're ner' as high the dead worm held firm in the grip of a small
bird's beak.

It's ours now to once and finally break loose all the chains and be
truly free.

Off our self-loving high horse, that hollow arrogant steed, is our true
mystery.